UTOPIA, OREGON

A NOVEL

By Eileen Pinkerton

2017

Pink Curtain Press

"Angel Band" by Jefferson Hascall, pub. 1860

"Bury Me Beneath the Willow" traditional, public domain

Cover photo by Bruce Harvey

Author photo by Theresa Casagram

VW Van by Samonberry

www.pinkcurtainpress.com

To the original insect judge

1

Everyone loves an earthquake

Scorpio lay splayed across his thin prison issue mattress reading a worn paperback. His leg draped over the edge of the bed, foot tapping the floor as he read. It was almost dinnertime. His cellmate had left for kitchen duty half an hour ago.

"Silverfish, 'hungry soul,'" he read aloud.

What about 'angry soul'? What about 'I don't belong here' soul? What about 'if I ever see Rocco again I'll kick his ass' soul?

He shifted on the mattress again and felt the slats digging into his back when the ground beneath the Walla Walla State Penitentiary began to shake. He threw his paperback to the floor, his interest in insects suddenly interrupted.

He lunged for the bars in the doorway of his cell and hung on. The floor heaved like an ocean wave; there was crashing and chaos everywhere. He pressed his face hard against the cold metal, trying to see beyond his space.

Scorpio pumped his arms as he held onto the bars, body rocking, throat constricted, as he let out a howl. He laughed so loud. He loved watching as the earthquake beat the hell out of this old building; *God, what a great day this was turning out to be.*

The ground swelled and rolled, men hollered throughout the building. A metal railing fell with a clang. Tiles crashed from the ceiling; the wall in the corridor cracked wide open.

Then came the silence.

Scorpio could feel his hands vibrating when he let go of the bars. He turned to survey the small room in wonder. The ceiling was caved in over the bunks, the toilet cracked and flowing across the cement floor. Another tremor hit.

That's when Scorpio saw daylight through a hole in the wall.

The sirens signaled a full lock-down. Scorpio squeezed through the new hole in his cell wall. He was on the lookout for any patrol that would try to stop him as he continued to move forward.

He saw fallen guard towers, and bodies crushed beneath crumpled sculptures of steel. Oh shit, there was the one-man torture chamber they called "The Mangler", crushed under his own tower. The Mangler would jump his own mother. He was bug-shit crazy and the guards let him get away with anything.

"That's what you get," Scorpio muttered to himself.

He ran past another crumpled tower. Sticking close to the wall, Scorpio crouched as he ran. He didn't see anyone in the yard and didn't take time to figure out why. He just kept running.

Dusk was falling on the onion fields around Walla Walla as Scorpio made his fateful journey across the prison yard.

He held his hands splayed, arms out to keep his balance as he kept vigilant on his trip across the compound. Scorpio's heart beat in his ears, and he tried to keep his head clear and focused. It was curiously silent as he raced for his freedom.

Then he heard the shouting begin from the other side of the cement walls of the prison.

Scorpio ducked and ran, waiting for the impact of the AR-15 shell to hit him from behind. Ignoring everything around him, he just moved forward; if he made it – sweet freedom, if he didn't, it would all be over quickly.

Cautiously he searched for any opening, any weakness in the wall. If the quake could create a crack in his cell wall, it had certainly made a way for him to get to the outside.

Scorpio's eyes darted back and forth, searching for a break in the outer wall. His breath was quick and shallow, his legs shook with adrenaline, his mind reeled like a junkie after a slam of crack. He focused all his energy on finding that opening.

Scorpio ran behind one of the fallen towers and discovered his hunch was right; the fence had been dragged and mangled when the tower went down. This was the weakness he was looking for. Scrambling over the maze of razor wire, he slipped through the break in the wall and never looked back.

Keeping to the ditch, he dodged the devastation around him. This was one bad-ass earthquake. Two of the legs of the water tower had buckled. It could collapse at any moment. Scorpio hoped so.

He headed away from the prison and toward the rural farms and fields that were only a few miles away. All he could do was keep moving away from the prison. If they found out he was gone, freedom would be a figment of his imagination.

Maybe it was anyway.

It was getting darker and Scorpio saw barns and houses in the distance. He was rustling through a cornfield, crouching as he went. A huge barn ahead would be his refuge and he made that his first goal. *Make it to the barn...make it to the barn.* He repeated this to himself as he focused on his first stop, still flinching at the thought of a bullet slamming into his back.

The barn would be his place to take a breather while he decided his next move. As he got closer, he saw a farmhouse too close to the barn. Shit. He made it to the back side and touched the rough boards with his hand as if to reassure himself it was not an illusion. Legs bent to make himself small; he froze in the dark for a moment to listen for danger. Peeking around the barn he saw the front porch 50 yards away, the steps were in splinters around the dirt yard, looking like debris from a shipwreck. Through the window, a man was pacing and talking on the phone; a woman was turning the knob on a transistor trying to find some news. The heaving mounds of earth rolled amidst the fields. When he turned his head, Scorpio could see that the east side of the barn had collapsed.

A bright light flashed suddenly from the porch and startled him. Scorpio's heart skipped a beat and he dove under an orange flatbed. A fat farm cat had set off the auto-light, and he watched as it walked into the kitchen where the front door hung askew. With relief, Scorpio rolled sideways to extricate himself from under the truck and then he saw it.

Oh my sweet Jesus, a clothesline. It couldn't be! This sort of thing only happens in the movies. No dogs barked, no women screamed, no shotguns rang out as Scorpio grabbed a flannel shirt and jeans off the line, ran to the barn and changed in a hurry. All around him, the fields had heaved from the wave of the earthquake. He tucked his orange jumpsuit under his arm and ran through the jagged field. Finding a crevice in the earth, he buried his discarded clothing. *Where would he go? Canada. He would sneak across the border into Canada and never be found.* Scorpio fell as the earth began to roll again with an aftershock. This time he rode out the quake flat on his stomach, fists clenching the earth. When it finally passed, he stood and shook himself, running his hands down his jeans to remove the debris, grateful for the darkness.

2

Scorpio jumps a produce truck

A produce truck had been on the road for most of the afternoon when the driver felt the call of nature. He pulled off the deserted road; he left the door hanging open as he watered the sagebrush.

Scorpio had finished the last bite of a sweet onion that he had pulled from a field when he heard a truck stop a few yards down the road. He looked up into the night sky and smiled, *I'm in a flippin' movie. I knew it.* Sneaking up to the truck while the driver wasn't looking, Scorpio hopped onto the back bumper. He caught his balance then dove into the load of iceberg lettuce.

How far would this truck go tonight? He positioned himself at the tailgate to watch for the truck to slow at a turn in the road. Not just yet, he thought, he wanted to get as far down the road as possible. The road was broken by the quake, but somehow this truck had managed to get through. There were no lights in the distance; the power was out all over.

The truck driver had been driving most of the afternoon, and now it was dark. He had to get his produce to Oregon by morning. Never mind that the roads had been damaged by the quake. Damaged? It was like trying to drive through a war zone. He couldn't even think of stopping until he got to Pendleton. The hot daytime sun would ruin his lettuce. He should be running a reefer, but he was just a farmer; he couldn't afford one. *Cover the produce with wet gunnysacks, that'll do 'er.* This load would bring him enough money to live on for a month; but he had to drive four more hours to pull it off. He lit a cigarette and opened the window.

3

How Scorpio found himself in jail

Scorpio waited for his chance to jump. He didn't want to lose this ride too soon, but he didn't want to get caught in the city when the truck stopped either. The lettuce was damp and leaves were sticking to his skin. Not that he wasn't grateful. He still felt his heart pound at the thought of what he had just done. Oh shit, what had he just done? If he got caught, it would be back to prison for him with more time added. But he still had ten years, and what if he got away with it? He didn't plan to let his guard down. Ever. He would need an ID; he would need a place to live and a way to make money. Well, Scorpio would cross that bridge when he came to it, there were plenty of people who lived on the street and he could spend the rest of his life on the down-low if it meant his freedom.

God, when was the last time he had been under the stars? How long since he had made a plan for his own life, eat what he wanted to eat or go where he wanted to go? He pictured his new life as he rode in the back of the farm truck; a new town, a new house, a woman. His own TV. He would be in charge of his life. He would start smoking. This time he wouldn't fuck it up. The whole damned world belonged to him.

He had gone over that dreadful night again and again. The cops grabbing and cuffing him as they threw him on the ground. There was a knee in his neck. He couldn't breathe. He couldn't move. He didn't do nothin', why did they do him this way? Shit. His face was in the rocks, they felt like barbed wire cutting into his skin. Lights were pivoting yellow and red, the sirens never shut up. Damn that Rocco, they were in trouble now. Up shit creek without a paddle.

When they threw him into the cop car, his clothes were torn and his face was wet with blood. He thought again of that moment when he could have changed his mind, do it all over again with a different outcome. Where would he be now, in his parallel life? The one where he didn't follow Rocco into the liquor store.

They had been in Rocco's car, cruising and partying, listening to Metallica, same as every other Saturday night, then Rocco was bored and he had to have his way. They pulled up to the store and opened the door.

"Come on, guys, we're gonna get us some tequila."

Rocco laughed and the guys followed along.

Rocco was the one with the gun in his pocket, he wouldn't have used it, but the judge didn't buy that.

Scorpio wandered to the back and began looking at the collector bottles; picking them up and putting them back down again.

He set down a decanter and had just begun to turn around when he was tackled from behind.

What The Hell?!

Cops filled the joint, and then he was grabbed and thrown outside.

Scorpio was an innocent bystander; Rocco had never even told the boys his plan. Now he was sentenced to 15 years. 10 more to go.

The truck slowed and Scorpio heaved his body over the high tailgate and held on, waiting to jump. He tensed his body and looked for a place in the ditch to roll but the farm truck turned onto the highway and sped up. Hanging on, he vaulted back over the tailgate into the pile of lettuce and laughed to himself. The farther away from Oniontown the better, he thought, and settled back for a ride. He was wet from the produce, but he felt safe for now.

4

Cricket gets invited to a contest

Cricket was checking the mail when his cell phone rang.

"You want me to do what, now?" he asked the man on the line. He handed his wife, Angeline the mail as he came into the house.

"Let me look at the calendar," Angeline was waiting to see who was on the phone.

"Should be a good weekend for us to come over, can I call you back?" He ended the call and stared at the phone for a minute before he realized his wife was asking him a question.

"That was a guy in Oregon. He wants me to come to his fiddle contest in August."

"But honey, you don't play the fiddle."

"I know."

"Why are we invited to a fiddle contest?"

"He's read my book and wants me to judge his Giant Insect Contest."

"Will you get paid?"

"Money, lodging, food, giant insects. Sounds like a perfect weekend."

She turned to the calendar and marked it down on the next page.

"Where are we going?" she asked as she wrote.

"Utopia, Oregon."

She raised one eyebrow and looked at him, "Okay, August 24, Utopia, Oregon."

"Hey, Cricket. I have an idea."

He looked at his wife over the sink full of dishes, hoping it had something to do with helping him in the kitchen.

"Let's go early to this Bug Contest and I'll see if I can do some tattoos and we'll get a little publicity for your book."

"It'll be like a vacation," he responded.

"That's what I thought!"

"Where are we staying, by the way?" she asked.

"Brad said they have a group of cabins on the festival property and we can stay in one of them."

"Call and see if we can go down early!"

"You finish these dishes, and I'll go get the phone," he said, drying his hands with the dishtowel.

5

How Angeline got kidnapped

At the age of 12, Angeline lived in a treehouse with her mom and Garcia. And she had never been to school. They lived near Chicken Creek in The Independence Mountains in Northern Nevada. She spent her days wandering the trails and beading jewelry to trade at Rainbow Gatherings. Angeline was home schooled because they moved a lot. They tried to stay away from Granny, but Granny found her wading in the water one afternoon.

"Hey, Angel," she heard her name before she realized someone was on the riverbank.

She turned and wondered how this lady knew her name.

"I just saw your mom; she told me you were here."

Angeline watched her from her place in the creek.

The lady in the jeans and white t-shirt sat down like she had all day.

"Do I know you?" Angeline asked her, already knowing.

"I'm your Granny." *Of course she was.*

Angeline had to get to her mom, fast.

Granny watched her. They smiled at each other.

"Well, it's good to see you. Let's go back to our place and you can see my jewelry," she climbed up the dirty creek bank and squeezed the water from the hem of her skirt as she spoke.

"Okay, I'm parked right at the road up there, you can ride with me back to your place."

Now Angeline wondered if Granny had really been there, did her mom say it was okay?

Was this her Granny, really? She walked to the car, intending to run at the last minute.

"I have some sandwiches in the car, we can eat before we go if you want."

Angeline thought it should be safe to eat a sandwich.

After they ate, Granny showed Angeline some pictures of when Angeline was a baby. She showed her pictures of her mom when she was a baby, too.

"Oh, honey, your mom was so smart! She always got the best grades in science. She wanted to be a nurse."

Angeline had never heard this.

"Let's go to the store and get some food to take to your place. We can have dinner together."

Angeline felt more comfortable after they had talked about her mom and all that. She got in the car and off they went to the store.

"I have a surprise for you, Angeline!" said Granny.

"You get to come to my house for two days and we can visit and bake cookies and you can play with my dog."

Angeline was excited and worried at the same time.

"Where do you live?"

"Not far."

They kept driving and driving.

6

In which Scorpio acquires a dog

The 1986 Ford 350 one-ton hummed down the highway, now that the highway was smooth, somewhere just the other side of the Oregon border. The power was on, the roads unbroken; the driver had finally gotten past the earthquake damage. The bulletins on the radio were continual; the quake was 7.0, with the epicenter being outside Walla Walla. The prison was damaged and a convict had escaped. The high school was destroyed beyond repair; however, there were no people in the school because it was after hours. The fatality count was already 112 and growing; there were rescue workers in the downtown area searching for survivors in the rubble. The truck driver's property was far north of Walla Walla; he wasn't worried about his farm or family.

Scorpio sure wasn't worried. The longer the truck went down the road, the safer he was. The destruction of the earthquake meant his freedom; he never deserved to be in the State Pen.

The truck slowed and Scorpio could see the sky become brighter with the city lights. Standing up to stretch in the back of the truck, he arranged the wet burlap around the lettuce and heaved himself back over the tailgate, looking for that final place to jump.

Low on the tailgate, hands steady on the truck, he crouched and held on. He had seen this done in the movies; you kept your body as low as possible and rolled when you landed. A cinch.

The road turned from asphalt to dirt as the driver took the farm-to-market road past fields and farmhouses. Lucky for Scorpio. When the farmer slowed to take the curve in the road he launched himself toward the side of the ditch bank and rolled. The landing was like crashing into a wall. It wasn't like you see in the movies. This was brutal. His body bounced and somersaulted in the soft dirt and flew over the ditch into a cornfield, dust flying. When he finally stopped careening down the edge of the field, he slammed into a barbed wire fence with a *No Hunting* sign.

Scorpio lay for a few minutes in the dirt, cheek pressed against the earth, breathing hard. He rolled over onto his back and looked at the night sky. It was hard to breathe. He knew he had at least one broken rib, but that didn't matter; nothing he could do about it now. His ankle was tender, too, probably a sprain. He ran his hands around his ribs and down to his ankle. Time to get up and get going. His arm was scraped up and bleeding. It was all just superficial, though. Life was still good; he was still free. But God, he hurt all over. It was time to figure out where to spend the night. Scorpio heard a scrabbling through the cornfield and froze to listen. He crouched down and made his breathing shallow.

The cornstalks rustled as whatever it was moved down the row. He could hear snuffling now. He reached slowly down and felt for a large rock that was glinting in the faint moonlight; he would bust it in the chops. The noise was coming closer in the dark but he couldn't figure out how to get out of the way without alerting the creature that he was there. He wasn't going to wait to be attacked, that wasn't his style. Scorpio winced as he held his hand up with the rock in his fist, poised to protect himself.

There was a burst of noise as the animal shot from the stalks and Scorpio saw a flashing of teeth as the creature launched itself onto his chest.

He lost his balance as he swung his fist at the dog's face. It backed off and was growling a warning, but Scorpio was too.

"Get the HELL out of my face!" he snarled at the dog in a low warning voice.

The dog sat suddenly on his haunches three feet away from him, looking at Scorpio with interest.

"Get AWAY. Go HOME!" he hollered and feinted with his rock fist.

The dog reared up as if to fetch.

"You IDIOT I'm not PLAYING with you!"

Pant, pant, slobber. It was a hound, but he didn't know much about dogs; he had never had a dog.

Relieved that he wasn't going to be attacked, Scorpio got up and brushed off his clothing then limped off to find a barn to sleep in.

Hound followed.

"Go HOME!" he pointed and commanded in a loud whisper.

Hound sat and stared.

"Oh my GOD. I can't have some idiot dog following me..."

Wait a minute, he thought, a guy who broke out of prison wouldn't have a dog and be wearing jeans and a flannel shirt. He would be running through the fields, hiding in barns and acting paranoid.

"Well, it seems as though you came along just in time. Come on, now. Come on," he slapped his leg.

They walked down the side of the road, one limping, the other happy to be going for a walk.

7

Scorpio rides the Starry Night bus

Scorpio hobbled along the farm-to-market road, looking for a place to lie down. He wanted to get another ride so he could get as far away from Walla Walla as possible, but he needed to rest his body. That's when he heard the rumble of a vehicle behind him. Should he hitchhike? The dog made all the difference, now he looked like a normal guy. He turned, saw a large vehicle, and stuck out his thumb, hoping they could see him in their headlights. Sure enough, the bus groaned to a stop and the driver unhitched the door and looked down at Scorpio.

He stood in the doorway and looked up at the driver. She was a big mama. She had a scarf tied around her hair, a purple blouse billowing over large breasts, and a big sparkly skirt flowing over the seat.

"Have a ride with us!" she invited.

She was driving a school bus; in the moonlight he could make out that it was painted with blue swirls. There were huge bundles strapped to the top. This could be interesting.

He stepped up the stairs, the dog following.

"Wacher dog's name?"

He stood next to her, hanging on to the pole.

"Juneau."

"Juno, mother of Mars," the woman replied.

"Right," he answered.

"Sit down, sit down. Welcome to Starry Night."

"Starry Night?"

"Van Gogh. You know, *Starry Night.* The famous painting," she explained.

"Okay," he rolled his eyes as he turned his back on the driver.

Juno got comfortable under one of the seats and Scorpio looked around. How could it get any better than this?

"Where are we going?"

"We're heading to Utopia. Just a few more hours down the road. Me and my friends go to the Barter Faire every year- we trade jewelry and mirrors and garlic and stuff."

"Hey, I used to go to Blue Lake as a kid," he felt his heart beat faster, "That's near Utopia." He could go out to the lake again and remember the good old days, maybe go fishing. He leaned his head back on the seat; he began to feel relaxed and it was warm. He started to doze as she talked. Things just got better.

8

Cricket & Angeline arrive in Utopia, Oregon

When Cricket and Angeline got to Utopia, it was late afternoon. They had flown to the Pendleton airport and rented a car to take them the rest of the way. Even though Angeline had a map, they still had trouble negotiating exactly where to turn on the road that led to the secluded town. They had never been to the Northwest before, but found the scenery very pleasant on this hot July afternoon. There were a lot of deer. At first, Angeline would shout out every time she saw one. Now they were trying to dodge them with their car, hoping not to hit one on the way to Utopia.

"Here! Here! Take this road," Angeline pointed to the right, finger to the windshield.

Cricket turned off the main road and saw a wooden sign that said 'Utopia, 10 miles'.

"They don't care if anyone finds them, do they?" he commented to his wife.

As they approached the town, they saw signs that said 'Barter Faire & Fairy Congress' they looked at each other. He was skeptical; she was excited.

"I am totally going to that!"

"I guess you could get a lot of business there," her husband replied.

She was thinking how much fun it would be to live like a hippie for the weekend. She guessed there would be psychedelic buses and women with colorful flowing dresses and skirts. Little children running around, and great music. Her husband was the serious one; he wasn't the all-out crazy artist like she was.

"Stop here at the gas station; I want to see the schedule. Let's get a newspaper!" Angeline was almost bouncing in her seat.

Cricket pulled into the station and they both got out and stretched.

A colorful bus pulled into the station to gas up, and two men with scanty beards and dreads disembarked. Some women and a few children followed behind.

Angeline and Cricket looked at each other. She smiled.

"Are you going to the Barter Faire?" Angeline asked one of the women.

They both turned toward her, "It starts tomorrow, but we're getting there early so we can get a good camping spot."

"How do you get there?"

The woman with the ring in her nose explained while Angeline observed the family. Cricket wrinkled his nose at the smell of old garlic and patchouli.

Angeline picked up some snacks while Cricket paid for gas and they took off again to find the Fiddle camp. He hoped the contest wouldn't be like the Barter Faire, but he was beginning to have his doubts.

They followed the directions from a piece of paper, and as they drove up the dirt road they came to a meadow with small cabins edging the field.

Cricket pulled up beside a white truck that was parked by the stage.

A man came out of one of the cabins and waved, then he crossed the meadow and introduced himself.

"I'm Brad," he wiped his hand on his jeans and held it out to Cricket.

"Thanks for letting us come early; we needed a break," Cricket said as they shook hands.

They stood by the stage for a while and talked, enjoying the summer day. They talked about Cricket's book, his research, and about the contest.

"My wife wants to go to the Barter Faire," Cricket announced as they walked across the meadow to the cabins.

Brad looked at Angeline. "Really? Bunch of hippies. Too many of 'em if you ask me. They take over the town and beg on the street."

The couple got very quiet. Cricket agreed but didn't say anything.

"Well, I could get some tattoo business," Angeline said.

Brad apologized, "Sorry, I go off sometimes and can't keep my opinions to myself." He explained how to get to the Barter Faire and told them to get settled in; he had an appointment to go to.

The cabin was small and cozy; fridge, bed, dresser. Like a motel room with a kitchenette.

"This is going to be great!"

They unpacked and went outside to explore the grounds.

9

Nurse Magpie

"Why the limp, honey?" The woman startled him awake with her question.

Scorpio was pretty sore; the pain had set in after sleeping in the bus.

"Fell off a ladder. Think I broke a rib, too."

She was slowing to a stop at the grocery store parking lot and it was morning. What a wonderful way to travel, the hours had drifted by, and he was anonymous on the bus.

This woman was really friendly to him and his dog. Scorpio looked out the window and wondered where they were now.

The parking lot was full of other buses and people were coming and going from the store. His injuries were a perfect excuse for him to stay on the bus. The other passengers barely gave him a glance beyond the head nod or 'good to meet ya, Mon'. *White people in dreadlocks?*

This Barter Faire sounded like a good place to hide out for a while.

After the passengers entered the bus with their organic snacks and took their seats, the Starry Night bus was once again on its way down the road.

Scorpio nodded off to the sound of conversations around him; the music in the CD player was a folk singer, droning in a predictable monotone.

When the bus stopped again, he saw they were parked in the middle of freakin' Woodstock. He slowly got up and waited for everyone else to disembark before he limped down the steps of the bus.

Juno followed him out to the grassy camping area where they had parked.

The driver set a chair out for him.

"You just sit now while we set up," she stood in front of him with hands on ample hips.

"So, I know your dog's name, what's yours?"

"Scorpio."

"Passionate but manipulative. I'm Magpie, attracted to bright shiny objects."

He looked at her with interest.

"Do you label or judge?"

"What do you mean?" she asked.

"Are you putting me in a category or judging me?"

"Both"

"I mean, you said that about my dog and me and then about you and shiny things. What kind of game is that?"

She bent down and patted his knee.

"I don't play games. Now hold down the fort while I get some wrapping for your ankle and ribs."

She got back on the bus and rustled around for something to help her new friend.

Everyone else was already setting up their tents and hauling gear back and forth, staking their claim on small patches of grass near the bus. Some planned to sleep on the bus that night. There were seven of them in all and everyone had been to this Barter Faire before, each of them had things to trade or sell. The musicians set up and soon had chairs in a circle near the side of the bus and were jamming. Fiddle bows were flying and guitars beat a fast rhythm to Sleepy Eyed John. Other folks stopped to listen and some began to dance. Scorpio watched with curiosity; this was all new to him; he couldn't believe the way his life had changed in 24 hours.

A young girl who was traveling with them sat down in the grass beside Juno and started to pet her. She got up and got a container of water and asked Scorpio if she could feed his dog.

"I ran out of food for her." Scorpio hadn't really thought about dog food.

The young girl ran off.

Magpie came back and wrapped his ankle.

"Stand up, now," she told him, "hold out your arms."

Stretching out the fabric, she wrapped it round and round his chest then secured it with a safety pin.

It felt good to be able to breathe. She handed him a pill.

"Take this, and relax while we finish setting up."

The little girl had returned with food for the dog, who wagged her tail at the attention.

Opening the brown paper bag, the young girl laughed as she squatted to pour the food into the hubcap.

"What kind of a dish is this?" she asked Juno.

She was wearing her favorite purple tie-dye dress. She and Magpie had made it. Her skinny legs stuck out from under the dress and were covered with matching purple tights. She was small for her age, but her big personality made up for it.

Scorpio did as he was told and soon his eyes were half closed, he was warm and safe and no one could get him.

10

Angeline "visits" Granny's house

Angeline had been bamboozled. Her Granny didn't take her back after the weekend. She let her guard down when they got to the house and she saw her room. Pure white bed-covers, dresser and curtains. Pictures on the wall of sunsets and trees and there was a birdhouse on the dresser, not like the ones you see in the hardware store. This one was covered with bark and moss and sticks.

"Let's go hang the birdhouse!" was the first thing Angeline said when she walked into her room.

They spent the weekend going to the park, looking through the attic at her mom's old stuff, reading at night from *Anne of Green Gables*.

Then on Sunday night, Granny had some news.

"Angeline, we need to have a serious discussion."

She looked up from the wildflower book she had been studying.

"Your mama said you could live here and go to school."

Angeline sat very still. Her mama said what? Was that the truth?

"I know it will be a hard transition for you, honey, but it will be for the best."

Oh, no, this woman was crazy after all. Angeline would have to be sneaky. She would have to make a plan to get back to her mom and Garcia without Granny knowing.

"Can I wait a few days to start, Granny?" she asked innocently.

"I don't see why not, we'll go down to the school the day after tomorrow."

Angeline didn't know how to get hold of her mom and Garcia. They didn't have a phone; they didn't get mail. The only thing she could think of was to send a letter to the general store where her mom went to get food and use the phone now and then.

The next day she wrote a letter and grabbed a stamp and envelope from Granny's desk; she dropped it in the mailbox down the street and hoped that they got it somehow.

11

Cricket & Angeline fight

"I can't believe you won't go to the Barter Faire with me!" Angeline was yelling at her husband.

"Just go. I'm staying here."

She walked out and slammed the door, then stood in the front yard.

The morning air was warming up, it was going to be a hot day and she was looking forward to going to the Faire. She wanted to see what happened at a Fairy Congress. She liked tattooing fairies.

That man! He knew she got lost easily; she didn't want to go to this gathering alone.

Realizing she had forgotten her things, Angeline turned around and snuck back in the door. Cricket was still in the bathroom, so she might get away with it. She slid the suitcase across the table quietly and as she grasped the handle, the whole contents dumped to the floor with a clatter. The clasp wasn't fastened.

"Why don't you get us some garlic while you're there?" he yelled through the door.

"Shut up, you jerk!" She gathered her gear and slammed the door again.

Driving down the dirt road, she thought about their relationship. He was adverse to that whole hippie thing. He was too scientific. She was artistic.

He had been ignoring her lately.

He started it when he left a mayfly in her suitcase yesterday. It was in one of those little Plexiglas boxes that he liked to use for his insect collection. Naive? That was infuriating. She wasn't naive. He didn't understand her. She was excited to meet new people and have new experiences. This whole vacation was for them to get away from their everyday life and have fun.

She had walked outside and dumped the mayfly. She wandered among the leaves and it didn't take long for her to find what she was looking for. She placed the tick in the box and left it on his pillow. *Stubborn.*

She slowed the car down and took some deep breaths, then turned on the music. *Crooked Still* changed her mood. With one eye on the road, she reached over and pushed the button on the glovebox and pulled out the crumpled map. She had to figure out how she was going to get to this thing without getting lost.

Passing the grocery store, she noticed all the colorful buses and realized all she had to do was follow one of them and she would be fine.

She circled back around and sat in the parking lot and watched the parade of people entering and leaving the store. Their vehicles were all loaded down with boxes, bags, and bundles.

Angeline started following a bus that looked like that Van Gogh painting, the one with swirling clouds and stars in beautiful blues and yellows. She had to back off when they got to the dirt road that led to the festival; the dust was churning behind the bus and getting into her car, even with the windows up.

The road was lined with buses and cars waiting to pay and park. As she got closer, she could see families and little children running and chasing each other. Barter booths were filled with beautiful wooden instruments, produce, and swaths of colorful fabric and jewelry. She heard music from circles of people jamming and she saw dancing; there were even people dressed up as fairies. Her heart was beating fast as she parked the car and walked through the crowds.

It felt like she had come home.

12

Angeline's Tattoos

Two women were sitting at the registration table; holding court. The first day of the Barter Faire had arrived. People were showing up and filling the meadows; there were no problems to solve at this moment. One of the women was putting last minute touches on the schedule of workshop speakers and music. The other was fielding questions from fairies, wood nymphs and pixies. It was going to be a great weekend.

"My name is Angeline," Angeline said shyly; she was standing in front of the registration table.

"My name is Sunbird, nice to meet you," Sunbird took Angeline's hand.

Angeline had laid out her painted suitcase, decorated with insects all over.

"I really wanted to meet you and just say this is awesome!" she began.

"Thank you. What's in the suitcase?" Sunbird asked.

"I'm a tattoo artist. I want to show you something."

She brought out Cricket's book.

Sunbird picked it up.

"My husband wrote this book about the symbolism of insects."

"See, beetles represent divinity and the gods," Angeline was explaining the concept of her husband's book, "and the wasp means royal queen."

The women were pointing at pictures in the book as they paged through it.

"Can I set up my tattoo equipment? Do I sign up with you guys?"

Sunbird set the book on the table and looked through the suitcase.

"Cool! I think you could totally set up by the Fairy Congress tents, there's one or two unused outlets up there."

The other woman picked up the book, "Daddy long legs: communally passionate. Oh, that's me," she said.

"I like the Egyptian beetle," said Sunbird.

"I've got a handout you guys can keep," Angeline handed them the pamphlets and closed up her suitcase with the book inside.

"I'll be seeing ya," with a backwards wave, she walked toward the circle of tents to find the power outlets and set up her tattoo station.

The two women were still looking at the handouts as Angeline wandered away.

13

Angeline meets Magpie at the Starry Night camp

Angeline set up at the back of the tea kitchen. There was plenty of space and she found a table to use along with two chairs. It was primitive, but she could make do.

The north side of the Fairy meadow had a large circle of tents with paths likes spokes in a wheel. The kitchen tent was set in the middle, with the tea kitchen, first aid tent, children's area, and craft tent in a circle around the outside.

Angeline watched the 3 Sisters Tea Company delivery as she set up her station. Cases of the tea were being carried down the path to the tea kitchen. This tea was a special Utopia blend for the Fairy Congress. It consisted of rose hips, lavender, mint, clover and chamomile. Organic and pesticide free.

Angeline arranged the handouts artfully across the table, placing Cricket's book front and center. There were also heavy three-ring binders with artwork to choose from. She had established a small gathering before she had even finished setting out all her display materials.

"Cool suitcase, man," said a passerby.

"What's this book about?" asked another.

"Would you trade for some jewelry?"

"Do you need a dress? I sew dresses," someone offered.

"Let me see your jewelry," Angeline said to a woman with a long blond braid. The woman with the long blond braid said she'd be right back, and went to go get some jewelry. The dressmaker showed a few dresses to Angeline.

A few hours later, she needed to get some food and take a break. Angeline had done a ladybug signifying luck and balance, and a locust signifying vagabond minstrel in trade for 2 swirly dresses and a wooden flute.

She passed a large group of children splashing and playing in the shallows of the creek which bisected the Barter Faire from the Fairy Congress. They were catching minnows and collecting rocks and cooling off on the sandy beach nearby.

Angeline crossed the parking lot to her car. She saw the colorful bus she had followed to the Barter Faire parked at the camp. In the spirit of camaraderie, she stopped in front of the bus to talk to the group of people. They were taking a break from playing music, so she took the opportunity to greet them.

"Hey, I'm Angeline. I followed your bus here."

"I'm Magpie, glad to meet you. You want to sit down?"

She sat with the group and admired the bus.

"Did you paint this?"

"Me and Deja and our group of Rainbows," she said. "It's the Van Gogh painting, *Starry Night*. What's in your suitcase, bugs?"

She laughed and opened the clasp.

"This is my tattoo kit."

"Oh, cool!" Everyone in the camp gathered around. Except Scorpio, he was dead to the world with his head back and his legs splayed in the lawn chair.

She explained about the language of insects and handed out the colorful pamphlets.

"You wanna trade some of our stuff for a tattoo?"

"Of course."

It was so lovely sitting amongst her new friends, she sat for a good long time and admired their clothing and handmade items.

"Where do you guys live?" she asked.

Scorpio was coming out of the fog of sleep when he heard their conversation. It was a pleasant day, warm and sunny; he had a good nap and his pain had gone down a few notches. Scorpio might not have anything in this world, but he had his freedom.

"We all live in different places and we get together once a year for this festival. Little Deja brought her fairy costume for the Fairy Congress tomorrow. Did you see the white flag circle and tent across the creek?"

"That's where my station is; I'm plugged into an outlet by the tea kitchen," Angeline said.

"We're about ready to start setting up our booth; I guess we'll meet you over there later. Did you get anything to eat?" said Magpie.

"I'm going to get something on my way. I'll see you later!"

Scorpio watched Angeline walk away with half closed eyes.

14

Cricket alone on their vacation

Cricket had the cabin to himself and he wasn't happy about it; this was supposed to be a vacation for the two of them. They came early to have some time together. And here was Angeline, running off to the Barter Faire, hanging out with hippies and wasting her time. There were so many great places they could hike together in the Blue Mountains. That's what he thought they were going to do.

Cricket unpacked his suitcase and noticed Angeline hadn't even touched hers yet. He peeked into her suitcase and saw the mayfly was gone. Well, she must have gotten the message.

She was totally naïve.

Hey, wait a minute, that same container was on his pillow. He opened it and found a tick. He took it outside and shook it roughly into the grass a few feet outside the driveway. Stubborn? What was he being stubborn about? She was crazy if she was putting the blame on him.

He looked up as Brad's truck pulled into the driveway and honked. He was in no mood for company but this was Brad's place, so he couldn't ignore him.

"How are you settling in?" he asked Cricket through the truck window.

"It's going great, thanks."

"I'm going into town, need anything?"

Cricket took a moment to think; there were things he needed.

"You can come along if you want."

"Let me get my wallet, I'll be right back."

On the ride into town, Cricket was unhappy that Angeline had left him stranded without a car, though he appreciated the lift from Brad.

"Wife using the car?" Brad asked.

"She's at the Barter Faire."

Brad snorted, "I got an extra car you can use while you're here if you want."

Cricket perked up, "I'll take you up on your offer."

"It's a deal, then," said Brad.

When they got to the local market, Brad pulled into a space and sat there for a moment, watching the hippies crossing the parking lot.

"I'll tell you, Cricket, this Fairy Party they have every year brings in the riff-raff. Not all of them go home. They hang around with their broken down machines. I've seen them sleeping in the library."

Cricket shook his head.

"Were you both raised on the East Coast?" Brad changed the subject.

"Yeah. We live in a little college town, brick homes, and cobblestone streets. You should see it. Angeline has to have her tattoo salon outside the city limits because there's no zoning for it in our town."

After they made their purchases, they met at the front of the store with their groceries. As they walked back to the truck together Brad commented, "See, the thing is, these people don't leave when the Faire is over. They stay and squat on abandoned property. They beg on the streets. Crime goes up when the Faire starts and stays up for months."

"I can see that," Cricket responded.

"Wanna get a beer?" Brad asked.

"Why not?" he agreed, it was not much past noon, but he was on vacation.

15

In which Cricket acquires a new friend & a job

Cricket and Brad sat in Three Finger Jack's watching the bartender wash the glasses.

"Angeline and I have been together since college," said Cricket.

"Well, you should know each other pretty well by now," Brad replied.

"I didn't know she would do something like this."

The beer commercial on TV distracted them for a moment.

Brad held up two fingers, signaling for a round of drinks.

"Tell me about your Giant Insect Contest," Cricket asked Brad.

"Well, I wanted to bring the love of insects to children. The fiddle contest runs from 9 in the morning until 7 at night. We take a break at noon for the insect contest. There will be about 50 kids waiting in line in front of the stage, and that's when you take over. You'll have an assistant and all the tools you need for judging. I've got microscopes, gram scales, measuring devices. We have lab coats and gloves, the whole enchilada."

"What kind of insects have you seen in the past? Anything interesting?"

"Someone brought an African Spiny Flower Mantis one year."

"*Pseudocreobotra ocellata* in Utopia?"

"Little Petey Larson's aunt sent an egg case from her mission home in South Africa, they hatched it here."

The bartender brought another round.

"First prize is a hot air balloon ride."

"Jeez, you guys are serious about insects around here. This is my kind of town. I'd like to set up a lecture and book signing. Any ideas?"

"Talk to Andrew at the Pub, they do a lecture the first Tuesday of every month. Also, The Trail's End Bookstore is always looking for authors to do book signings; I bet you could get in on that."

Cricket and Brad set their empty glasses on the counter. Brad slapped his hands on the bar and startled the few customers that were watching the game. "Let's go get that car for you," he said, and they paid the tab and walked into the bright sunlight.

Later, as Cricket drove the little Subaru down the dirt road to their cabin, he was thinking about his situation. What a great turn of events. He had two possibilities for lectures. And he had been here less than 24 hours.

Gathering his stuff, he changed into slacks and a polo shirt and was out the door in 20 minutes. As Cricket drove through downtown Utopia, he decided to check with the bookstore first. Cricket parked and went inside.

A young woman looked up as Cricket approached the counter.

"Hi, my name is Cricket Sibley and I would like to talk to the person in charge."

"That would be me," she said abruptly, grabbing a handful of books to put on the shelf behind her.

"Could I just see that book for a minute?" he reached out toward the stack she was holding.

She hesitated.

"Really," his hand was stretched out toward her.

She turned slowly toward Cricket and let him take the book off the top of the pile.

"This is my book. I wrote this."

She dropped the rest of the pile on the counter. Cricket had her attention, now.

"I love this book," she exclaimed.

He was holding the book up and showing her his author photo on the flyleaf.

Now the woman had opened a drawer and was rummaging through it in a sudden flurry of activity.

Pencils flew and tiny pads of sticky notes cascaded from beneath the counter.

Cricket watched with interest.

"I wonder if I could arrange to come for a lecture and book signing," he tried to get her attention.

"I just need to find a pen," she took one out and scribbled on a nearby invoice. "Just hold on, I've got one here somewhere," she implored. Scribble. Toss. Scribble.

"Aha!" She thrust the pen at him.

Startled, he pulled away.

"Your autograph," she explained.

He laughed, "You startled me."

She watched as he signed his name in the front of the book.

Satisfied, she dug under some papers and found her calendar and wrote his name in big letters on the first week of September.

"I'll call the radio and the paper right now and we can start publicity. Thanks so much for coming in, this is awesome!"

He left the bookstore with a jaunty step and smiled all the way to the car.

16

Cricket's new resolve about his wife

Cricket returned to the cabin wondering when Angeline would be back from her little day trip. He wanted to tell her about his gig at the bookstore. He was going to try to get on the Pub lecture schedule later. Brad had been encouraging and the Giant Insect Contest sounded like fun.

Everything seemed to be going his way for once.

Cricket saw the small insect box sitting on the kitchen table and held it in his hand. He remembered their fight this morning before she drove off.

Oh yeah. Cricket wasn't really mad anymore, he should let her do what she enjoyed doing with her day. Why was he trying to control her? They each had their own interests, would she try to stop him from his writing, or his lectures? When she got home he would apologize.

There was still a lot of daylight left, so Cricket changed into jeans, t-shirt and tennis shoes and set out across the field to see what kind of interesting things he could find; he was determined to enjoy this bright sunny day. Cricket walked as far as the river, sat on a rock and took off his shoes and socks. He was going to see what was in the creek and cool off a little. He took a little insect box from his pocket. What did he really want to say to her? He was not good with words, or expressing himself to her.

But he wanted to let her know he respected her right to live her life in a way that made her happy. Just because they were married didn't mean they had to be connected at the hip.

He just wished they could get along.

As he walked back to the cabin, Cricket stopped here and there to poke in the grass and check under the tree bark to see what kind of interesting insects he could find. When he got in the door, he saw what he needed near the kitchen sink. Cricket opened the little box and dropped in a fruit fly.

Life is fleeting.

17

In which Angeline tattoos Magpie

Angeline sat at her table with a box of treasures beside her. She traded the box from a guy who had sold all his apples. The box was now filled with two dresses, a mirror in a stained glass frame, a chicken clock, a flute and an amber earring and necklace set. She had tattooed people with two fairies, a ladybug and a Japanese beetle. She was conferring with Magpie now.

"I want a magpie right here," she pointed to her shoulder. "He will be flying toward my back and there will be another magpie waiting on a branch with flowers."

"The magpie is a symbol for creative expression," said Angeline.

"Yes, and a love for bright shiny objects" finished Magpie. They laughed.

"How did you become a tattoo artist?" Magpie asked.

"I left home as soon as I could," she began, "I was hanging out with the dishwashers downtown, then I picked up a job at a bar."

She was arranging tools and picking colors for the flowers as she talked.

"One of my new friends worked in a tattoo studio, and he agreed to apprentice me. At first it was rebellion, but then I fell in love with the intimacy of it. Many of my clients are scarred on the inside, and this expresses their joy, or memories of loved ones, a birth of a baby. It's a celebration of life and personality."

"How did you and Cricket meet?" Magpie asked.

"He was in his last year of college studying entomology. We went out on one date and I just never went home. No loss, I was couch surfing anyway."

It took her about two hours to complete the tattoo for Magpie. She was enjoying their easy camaraderie.

Angeline held up the hand mirror for Magpie to see her new tattoo.

"This is awesome," she exclaimed and hugged Angeline gently. "I better go," she said, "I've got to take my turn at the booth."

As Magpie walked away, Angeline turned to the folks waiting near the table, "I need to take a break," she told them apologetically.

She wanted to go to the yoga tent and stretch, to walk around and see some more booths and listen to the jam sessions going on around the campground.

She set her suitcase in the box of treasures and carried them to the car before she set out for the yoga tent.

On the way to the car, she walked by the Starry Night bus again. This time that young man was awake and sitting in a lawn chair petting his dog. He had been asleep earlier, but she barely noticed him, there was so much going on. The musicians had gone and the guy and his dog were hanging out at the bus.

He watched her as she walked past; she looked his way and felt uncomfortable and looked away again.

"Hey, I can help you carry your box" a girl came running up to Angeline and held out her arms.

"Okay, you can carry the box and I'll carry the suitcase," she answered.

They had about 50 feet to go.

"My name's Deja, I'm 10," the girl told her.

"You are very helpful, Deja. Thank you."

They set the box and suitcase in the trunk and stood by the car for a moment.

"Are you here for the Fairy Congress or the Barter Faire?" asked Deja.

"Both," said Angeline.

"I can't wait for the Fairy Congress. I brought my wings and antennas," she said.

She skipped in a circle while she talked, arms out and then down again.

"I'm going to the yoga tent. Have you ever done yoga?"

"Yes. That dog's name is Juno."

This girl switched subjects like a traffic light switched colors.

"Beautiful dog," Angeline laughed, trying to keep up with Deja.

As they passed the Starry Night bus again, Deja ran up the stairs to the bus, then stuck her head out and yelled back, "Wanna see my costume?" Angeline laughed and waited outside for the little girl.

She stood in the camp waiting, that guy was still sitting in the lawn chair. He was reading now and looked up.

"Hi there," he nodded to her.

"Hi," she felt self-conscious. It was the way he was looking at her.

He held out his hand and she held out hers, "My name's Scorpio," he offered.

She jerked her hand from his and then was ashamed of her reaction. *What was that all about?*

"Sorry," she said and reached out her hand again. She felt unsettled in his presence, but it wasn't rational. It was like the opposite of what she felt with Magpie. He stared at her as he took her hand again.

What was that all about? He thought.

Deja came out of the bus with her outfit on, looking ready to cavort with a whole band of fairies.

"Oh, you look wonderful, Deja. You want to walk with me?"

She squealed and skipped around Scorpio's chair. She bent down and patted Juno on the head three times "One! Two! Three!"

"Let's Gooooo!" She flung her arms out and ran while Angeline laughed.

"Nice to meet you," she fibbed.

"You too," *he wanted her.*

Scorpio, the scorpion. The symbol of retaliation, aggression, deceitfulness. She didn't trust him.

18

Scorpio steals money and wanders the Faire

Oh God, being in prison for five years had made Scorpio hungry. Hungry for everything he had missed. All these things that had been taken from him were now displayed before him like a banquet. He wanted to eat, he wanted to drink, and he wanted Angeline. It had been so long since he had seen or touched or smelled a woman, just to hear the sweet voice of one, to be in her company, near enough to caress her skin. Oh, his mind raced ahead of his sensibilities. *Whoa now, rein it in,* he told himself, *this filly will be worth the wait.*

Scorpio needed another change of clothes and he needed food. He needed money. Walking on his injured ankle was a hardship, his ribs still hurt if he coughed, but he realized now they were only bruised. The pill had worn off, probably a Valium. Scorpio stood carefully; he was going to look for some more. Using the railing, he helped himself up the bus steps for a look around. These people were sure a trusting lot; all their possessions were sitting on the seats for anyone to dig through.

He spied a green canvas duffel bag that had some clothes in it; he knew he couldn't just start wearing someone else's clothes. Ah, what have we here? A stash box. This would make him feel better. Scorpio pocketed a few buds for himself after carefully wrapping them in paper. What's this? A roll of bills. Smiling, he peeled a twenty and added that to the bud in his pocket.

Bingo! Scorpio found several boxes of food toward the back. Yogurt, goat cheese. These people don't eat like normal people, but he was hungry. Rummaging through the boxes, he found a spoon and picked up one of the containers of yogurt. Spew! Sour! Scorpio wiped his mouth, then he unwrapped some cheese and broke off a piece. Jeezus, it tasted like gym socks. What else was in here? He looked in the boxes. Carrots. Huh, finally something normal. Potatoes, garlic, olive oil, granola bars. He grabbed some granola bars, carrots, and an apple. That should tide him over until he could make his way to one of the cooking tents. Scorpio was going to buy a good meal and some clothes. He left the bus and made his way across the grassy parking area toward the smell of food.

Scorpio passed a man in a black derby hat playing a concertina with a brown pygmy goat tied to a tent post. Juno sniffed at the goat but she was turning out to be a mellow dog, nothing really fazed her. Good girl. Scorpio kept following the smell and knew there was a grill somewhere nearby; he could see the smoke now. His appetite was returning and his snacks were gone. Scorpio planned to eat until he couldn't move.

Speaking of appetite, here comes a sweet thang. *This gal is asking for attention and I know just how to give it to her.* A redhead was wearing an outfit straight out of a John Wayne movie, and what do you know? She was looking right at him as she walked toward him. Her tits were mounded up almost to her neck under her lace up top and her skirts were full and multi-layered. Except for the part that was gathered up high to the waist to show off her tan leg.

She looked straight into Scorpio's eyes as she approached, "Wanna smoke a bowl?" she asked.

He smirked and kept nodding as he and Juno followed her to the stand of trees north of the kitchen tents. There were other smokers under the trees, standing around in groups, the whole forest smelled like ganja. She took his hand and led him to a spot in the pine needles and took her pipe out of the shoulder bag she had slung across her body. He recognized the

Virgin of Guadalupe on her bag. Gallo, his roomie had sketches of her on the wall by his bunk. Jeez, what was Gallo doing right now?

19

Scorpio & Melody

They sat on stumps in the grove of trees. It wasn't like they couldn't smoke out in the open; this place was like Woodstock.

"So what's your name?" said the redhead.

"Scorpio."

"Oooh, that's awesome. I'm Melody."

Scorpio inhaled as much as his lungs would hold, he passed the pipe and watched Melody suck on the pipe, holding a lighter over the bowl.

"Where do you live, Melody?" he asked. She wasn't Angeline, but she would do.

"Montana," Melody said, breathing in while she spoke.

"This is a long way from Montana."

After a pause, Melody let out the smoke with a rush.

"I come every year. I make renaissance clothing. If I hit all the fairs and markets, I can make a whole year's wages during the summer."

"Where are you from?" she asked.

"Walla Walla. I broke out of prison during that earthquake."

"Wow, I heard about the earthquake. Why were you in prison?" Melody acted like she talked to prison escapees all the time.

"I was with a group of guys and one of them decided to hold up a liquor store. They got me as an accessory. I didn't even know what was going on," Scorpio's voice sounded whiny.

"How long were you in there?" Melody was looking straight into his eyes again.

"Five years."

They stared at each other for a moment; a buzz was starting to build that didn't have anything to do with the pot.

Scorpio reached out and ran his finger down her bare arm and watched her shiver. Taking the pipe from Melody's hand, he asked her, "Would you like to see our bus?"

Melody let him take her hand and guide her through the trees out to the meadow that led to the parking lot. No one paid attention as the two wandered across the grass to the privacy of the big blue bus.

Scorpio stopped outside the bus and turned facing Melody, placing his hands on either side of her ribcage.

"Do you like this, Montana?" he brought his lips very gently to hers and barely pressed against them. She held very still.

He increased the pressure of his hands on her ribs and slid them down to her waist. Increasing the pressure of his lips on hers, he began to suck on them one at a time.

"How about this?"

"Mhmm," she pressed into his body.

His hands rode up and down, ribs to waist and back again. They slid their bodies back and forth in a gliding motion, dancing a slow languid dance.

He took both her hands and guided them to his zipper and held them there for a moment. "I've got something for you," he said.

"Five years?"

He smiled at her and nodded.

"Well, what are we waiting for?"

20

Angeline's flashback

Angeline was following the smell of freshly baked bread when she saw the Okanogan Baking Company sign. She laughed out loud when she saw a man and two women behind the table juggling dinner rolls. They tossed them to and fro as the crowd watched, and then they switched places as they juggled. After a few moments, one of the women caught a roll and took a bite before she passed it on. They all began to toss and bite, toss, bite. The group reacted with laughter as the rolls got smaller and smaller and finally disappeared. With the last bite, all three turned to the crowd and took a bow. Amid the clapping of the appreciative audience, hands reached out to buy bread and cookies that were on display at the counter.

Deja jumped up and down which made her fairy wings flap as she waited for Angeline to hand her an oatmeal cookie.

"That was cool!" She took a bite. "I wanna juggle! Can you teach me to juggle?" she asked Angeline.

Angeline set her hand on Deja's head, avoiding the antennae. "I don't know how. Let's find someone to show us."

They wandered around and looked at the booths. There were musicians, fortunetellers, stilt walkers, and face painters. There were some jugglers ahead, with circles made of rope in front of a booth. Jugglers were tossing various objects in the air and attempting to catch them.

"I think we've found it, Deja."

The little sprite jumped into the middle of a circle and picked up some scarves. She watched a teenager for a few moments and then tried it for herself.

"Watch, watch, watch! I'm juggling!" Deja's chin was tilted toward the sky, her eyes focused on the colorful scarves.

"I'm watching, I can see you! Good job!" She had become attached to this girl already. What a sweetie.

Something about the way the scarves floated and the way that Deja was dressed made her think of a memory she hadn't had in a really long time.

It was when she was living at her Granny's. She turned her head to distract herself from the memory; *it's all in the past. You're safe here at the barter Faire in Utopia Oregon.* A counselor told her to do this when she felt anxious. *You are an adult; you are eating a roll and watching jugglers.* She tried to bring herself back to the moment so the memories would stay deep down and not affect her.

"Deja!" she said this louder than she meant to.

The little girl looked up at her, startled. Her scarves floated to the ground.

"I'm going to make my way to the yoga tent, I'll see you later sweetheart."

"Okay, see ya!" Deja waved excitedly.

Yoga would be soothing if she could make it to the tent. She could stretch her body and clear her mind. Angeline continued to distract herself as she made her way through the crowd of people.

When Angeline got there, she took off her shoes and left them with a dozen other pairs sitting outside.

There was a young woman up front with impressively long blond dreadlocks sitting with her legs crossed holding a flute in her lap. The yoga instructor sat beside her and they were talking quietly, heads together.

Angeline was delighted to see Magpie sitting alone near the middle of the tent. She took a place next to her and Magpie patted her on the knee and leaned toward her.

"Angel, we meet again."

Angeline smiled as tears brimmed in her eyes.

"Magpie," she whispered back.

There was a respectful hush in the tent. Some people were talking quietly between themselves. The peacefulness inside the tent was a stark contrast from the commotion outside.

"My name is Aspen," the instructor began as she unfolded herself gracefully into a standing position.

"This is Mantis," *Spiritual Power.*

The flute player gave a slow smile.

"Please stand with me and we will begin with the Sun Salutation."

Mantis played a quiet, breathy flute and Angeline became lost as she concentrated on breathing and body movements.

"Hands in Namaste prayer position."

Angeline turned her body slowly and moved her arms as the instructor led in her slow calm voice.

"Inhale. Exhale. Stretch your arms up."

"Angel, come on out to the garden with me, we'll check on those tomatoes," her Granny called up the stairs.

Angeline was watching out the window, she had been running her hands through her grandmother's scarves, wondering if her mom would come for her. Did she get the letter? Did she really give permission for Angeline to live with Granny? Had she been kidnapped? Her Granny was really nice, but she wanted to be with her mom and Garcia. She was afraid to go to school.

"Coming!" Angeline carefully draped the colorful scarves over the dresser and ran down the stairs and through the house into the back yard to meet Granny in the garden.

As they searched for ripe tomatoes and talked, Angeline saw a man standing at the back gate.

"Granny, someone's here," she said.

Granny stood up and walked to the gate.

Angeline continued to kneel in the garden by the tomato plants, as she watched the grownups talk. She couldn't quite hear what they were saying, but she hoped it had to do with her going back to her mom and their tree house. Angeline didn't even have her things with her.

Their voices got louder.

"Hazel, you know you have to let me in."

Granny stopped talking and opened the gate.

The man walked right up to the garden and was looking at Angeline.

"Is your name Angeline?"

Angeline stood up and looked at him. Maybe her mom sent him.

"Yes," she replied.

"Can we all go inside?" The man looked at Granny, who nodded.

Angeline left the tomatoes and dusted off her knees with her hands as she followed the adults up the back stairs and into the cool house.

"Look, Hazel, here's the deal," the man said.

"I got a call from Angeline's mother this morning. We need to take care of this."

Adrenaline surged through Angeline's little body. Her mom had gotten the message. She sat down and bobbled her knees, she bit her nail and listened.

"Bill, they're living in a tree house for God's sake. Squatters. In the National Forest. She's never been to school." Granny's face got red and she slapped the table flat handed.

Bill held his hand up to her and said, "I know the situation," he looked at Angeline and looked at Hazel.

"Your Mother loves you, Angeline. She has really missed you."

Granny wiped her eyes and put her hands in her lap. She turned to her granddaughter, "Angel, can you go upstairs for a little while? We'll call you down when we have this settled."

"I think I should stay here and listen. This is about me, this is my life."

"You're right," Bill answered.

"So." He began.

He was silent for a moment. He looked at Angeline and hesitated.

"It will be best for everyone if you stay here with your grandma and go to school."

"Now stretch your left arm slowly across your body and begin Shevatsna," Aspen said calmly.

Tears were dripping down Angeline's face. She was safe. She was in the yoga tent.

"Slowly bring your awareness back to the room-"

Magpie heard Angeline give a sharp intake of breath and looked beside her to see what was wrong. She rolled over until she lay facing her friend.

Magpie laid her hand on the side of Angeline's head and looked into her face and whispered, "Everything's going to be okay."

21

Scorpio gets dissed twice

Scorpio walked off the bus hungry as a bear. He wanted some real food. His hunger sharpened by the pot and the good bang he had given that girl. He was on top of the world. He hadn't felt like this in years.

"Hey, Serpico," the girl called from the open bus window.

Serpico? He turned to see what she wanted.

"Bring me back something to eat, would ya?"

He raised his eyebrow at her disrespect, "Get your own," he called back to her and walked off.

With $20 in his pocket, he got to the bread jugglers booth and bought a roll. When he got to the barbeque tent, he caught sight of Angeline. Oh, she was fine. He was going to get some of that next. She disappeared into the yoga tent before he could reach her.

He could wait.

Scorpio felt a body bump into him on the fairway. "Hey, Pard!" Scorpio grabbed the guy by the forearm and clenched it tight. The guy jerked away and stepped back. "What the HELL?!" The confused man wrenched his arm from Scorpio's grasp.

"Watch where you're walking!" Scorpio said as he took off for the barbecue tent grumbling to himself. These people better watch out, disrespecting him. He didn't stand for that.

22

Cricket at the Pub

Cricket spent the afternoon and evening alone. He had a car now, but didn't feel like going anywhere. He wanted to see his wife. Had she said when she'd be home? He couldn't remember. Cricket tried her cell a couple of times but she didn't answer. He had forgiven her earlier in the day, but was getting irritated again. He didn't know anybody here. What was he supposed to do? Was it wrong to want to do things with your wife?

Cricket would make her stay with him tomorrow. This was their vacation. He was getting hungry and decided to drive into town to the Pub for dinner. Maybe he could find Andrew and set up a lecture. Angeline would come home and find him gone. Well she deserved it. It would serve her right.

He sat in the Pub drinking a beer and watching baseball, Cubs v Royals. Cricket liked baseball; his evening was getting better. The waitress came around to take his order.

"Is Andrew around?" he asked.

"He'll be here in a minute. He's just pulling in."

"Thanks."

Cricket ordered his food, a buffalo burger with aioli mayonnaise and a side of sweet potato fries. What a weird town this was turning out to be. He couldn't figure out if it was pretentious or down-to-earth. There were all kinds of really thin people obsessed with riding bikes. He knew how much those bikes cost. Seriously? He saw signs for the salmon reclamation celebration and he saw a huge health food store downtown. It looked like a supermarket. Cricket had never seen a yurt except in National Geographic Magazine. There was a whole subdivision of them up Bear Creek Road. These Yurties wore tie-dye and their children never combed their hair. Did they even go to school? He thought not.

When he was in the grocery store earlier today Cricket saw a dad with his sons. One of them was running up and down the aisle with a plastic water blaster gun, "Bang bang bang bam bam bam!"

"God, shut your kid up," he mumbled to no one in particular.

"Dad, dad, can we get this? Can I have it?"

Cricket watched as the dad had set his hand on his son's shoulder and said, "Now son, you know how we feel about plastic in the house."

Cricket had to turn away with a guffaw. No plastic in the house? He had never heard that one before.

23

Booking the Pub

"I'm glad to meet you," the owner of the Pub approached Cricket and held out his hand. "My name is Andrew."

"My name's Cricket," he introduced himself and shook the man's hand.

The owner sat down at the stool next to Cricket's.

"Do you have an opening in your Tuesday lecture series? I'd like to make a presentation."

Andrew called out to the waitress, "Hey, bring the calendar."

"So, what do you want to lecture about?" he turned back to Cricket.

The bartender set a beer in front of them while they waited for the waitress to bring the calendar.

"*The Language of Insects.* It's a book I researched and wrote about the symbolic meaning of insects. I have my degree in entomology, and I began to notice something about the insect world. Through the ages, there have been insects in dream interpretation, and identified with gods, and I noticed that each type of insect has their own characteristics. They become symbols, and I have seen that each insect has their own meaning."

The bartender commented, "What do you mean?"

Cricket answered, "You give someone flowers when you want to tell them how you feel, right? A yellow rose means friendship and a red one means romance. Okay, so this is a different way of speaking. You could give a firefly to someone and that means 'playful'. You could get a tattoo of a ladybug for good luck."

"That's cool," Andrew was leafing through the book with interest.

"I've got a lecture at the bookstore in two weeks."

"Well, I'm interested, but I don't know if we have room on the calendar," Andrew said.

The waitress arrived, walking toward them with the book open, finger running down the page.

"We have a spot for the first Tuesday in September," she told Andrew.

"Let me see that," he flipped the pages.

"Will you be here September 5th?" he asked.

"Well, the contest is the 27th, so I don't see why we couldn't hang around a few more days," Cricket told him.

"Okay, then, you're on for the 5th," Andrew finished his beer and set it down on the bar.

"See you," he said.

"Nice to meet you," said Cricket.

"So tell me more about your bug book," said Patrick, the bartender, as he rinsed bar glasses in hot water. He wiped his hands and motioned, "give it here."

Cricket used to be offended when people called it the bug book. He was used to it now.

"The way I see it, there are many different ways to communicate."

Cricket could tell that Patrick was interested, not just faking it, so he went on.

"I began to research the history and symbolism of insects. They are found in Egyptian mythology, dream interpretation, ancient writings. I decided to put them all together in a book that would be like the language of insects."

Patrick had his elbows on the bar and was turning the pages of Cricket's book.

"See, a moth, for instance represents masculine wisdom."

He turned a few pages and then held the book up to read it.

"This is cool!" Patrick exclaimed. "Hey, Sherry, check this out."

She stood alongside Patrick.

"Look at this, a spider is supposed to be a 'creative deceiver'."

"Here's you, Sherry, 'lice: pay attention to me'."

She slapped his arm playfully, "That's not true."

"So what do you do with this information?" Patrick asked, turning back to Cricket.

"This information can be used for dream interpretation, or as another way to communicate with others. My wife does insect tattoos for people who want to express themselves through insects." Cricket answered him,

They talked some more until Cricket was done with his meal. Looking at his watch, Cricket realized that Angeline was probably home by now, so he left to spend the rest of the evening with her.

24

Angeline's recurring dream

Angeline came from the tent with the same old question, what was wrong with her that her mom had given her up so easily? She was always helpful and stayed out of the way and kept to herself most of the time. She didn't ask much of Mom and Garcia. They all seemed to get along. So why had her mom given her away to Granny?

After hearing the decision, Angeline had run up the stairs to her bedroom and thrown herself in bed. She sobbed there, alone, the rest of the day. Finally she had exhausted herself and fell asleep. Angeline never received a letter or phone call. It was as if Angeline had dropped off the end of the earth.

That's when she had the dream the first time.

Angeline was traveling on a bus alone. The first stop was an old deserted gas station. Where the pumps used to stand there was a pile of rubble-rocks and dirt. Caution tape was strung everywhere. Angeline walked into the station and saw food behind the glass counter, but it was locked. There was no one there to help her.

She was alone.

The bus was waiting and Angeline knew she only had a few minutes. She kept looking for someone to help her but no one was around. On her way out of the station Angeline saw another display counter. This one had a little tiny label she couldn't quite read.

Next to it, captured on a pin was a wingless gray bug.

A silverfish.

Angeline stood outside the yoga tent for a few moments and blinked her eyes to adjust to the bright sunshine. It was time to check out the Fairy Congress. She needed a little fantasy to shake these memories.

She crossed the creek on the little carved bridge and wandered toward the circle of white flags. There was a tent set up with tiny white lights scattered across the canvas. The poles were real cedar with strings of flowers wound around each one. There were musicians playing a concertina and a fiddle. Angeline watched Mantis, the yoga flute player, walk across the meadow and join them. Chairs were scattered around the field and people were sitting and visiting while others had formed a large circle and were keeping a balloon aloft that had been painted to look like the earth. They were laughing and pushing up with their hands as the earth balloon rose and fell in lazy bounces from hand to hand.

"Angeline," called a voice from behind her.

Angeline turned around and saw Scorpio with his hand raised in greeting. She felt odd. This guy was creepy. He looked perfectly normal, but she had this drowning sensation when he was around.

"Hello," Angeline said noncommittally. Scorpio stood too close to her, gazing at her as she watched the group keeping the earth aloft.

"This is a real fun time, huh?" He tried to start a conversation.

"Mhmm, yeah," Angeline didn't really look at Scorpio, but she was too polite to move away.

"So how much for a tattoo?"

She didn't look at him as she spoke, "Depends on what it is."

"What do you think I should get?"

"Do you have any tattoos already?"

"Come on over to the bus and I'll show you," he leaned toward her and whispered in her ear.

Angeline looked at Scorpio, her face registered alarm, "Uh, no."

He laughed, "I was just kidding," he lied.

"Come and find me and I'll see if I have time later today or tomorrow," she didn't realize she was coming back the next day until she heard herself say these words.

"I look forward to it, Angeline." Scorpio put his hand on her shoulder as he said this, then he turned and walked off.

She felt a shiver.

Angeline decided to leave. The peaceful moment at the Fairy meadow was over. She began to make her way over the carved bridge back to the parking lot. This was the photo that made the front page of the local paper that week; Angeline was holding up her skirt with one hand, the breeze caught the ends of her hair, and in the background you could see the group with their hands in the air, the earth balloon floating toward the sky.

25

In which Angeline comes home and tells Cricket her story

Cricket heard a car coming down the road. He had only been home about a half hour. He came out onto the porch step and watched the car pull into the driveway.

"Well, there you are" Cricket called when Angeline got out of the car. He sounded accusing, even to himself, he walked out to meet her and wrapped his arms around his wife in greeting.

She faked a smile, "Yes, here I am."

"I'm really glad you're home," his voice was sincere as he spoke the words.

Angeline stood there, numb in his arms and couldn't speak. She began to cry. It was safe here in her husband's arms.

"What is it? Angeline?" Cricket kept one arm around her and led her into the cabin, his head bent toward her.

Cricket sat Angeline down on the bed. He knelt down and took off her shoes, then brought her some tissue. He took hold of her ankles tenderly and brought them up onto the bed.

He brought her a cup of water, then sat with her, stroking her hair until she had finished drinking it. Angeline rolled over and went to sleep. He folded the blanket over her and watched as she slept.

Later, Cricket sat outside as the sun was going down. He made Angeline some chicken on the grill and was reading a novel he had found in the cabin.

Cricket anxiously waited for his wife to wake up. He was worried about her, but didn't want to disturb her.

Cricket checked on Angeline again and found her lying with her eyes open.

"Are you hungry, I made you some dinner."

She looked at him.

He handed her the cup of water. Angeline sat up and drank a few sips.

"I remembered about my Granny. That day she took me to her house."

Angeline's face contorted in pain and quickly recovered.

"I was at the river, and she just appeared with her big car." Angeline took a big shaky breath.

"Granny talked me into getting into her car and said I was going to visit her for the weekend. I should never have gotten into the car with her. It was my fault. I never saw my mom again."

She wiped her tears with a Kleenex.

"I sent my mom a letter to the little store down the road from our treehouse. Then a man came to the gate while we were in the garden. He said I had to stay with my Granny and go to school."

Cricket had heard this story before, but whenever he asked her about it, Angeline would shut him out.

"I can't figure out if my mom was trying to get rid of me, or if Granny kidnapped me," she looked at him as if he had the answer.

Angeline sighed, "I missed my mom so much. That's when I started having that same dream." She told him again about the bus, and the empty gas station and the food out of her reach and the silverfish with a label she couldn't read.

"Silverfish?" he asked.

"Hungry Soul," they both said at the same time.

"So what were you doing in the river when your Granny showed up?"

"I don't really remember. Wading around."

"How old were you?"

"I think I was 12. Yes, because I started in the sixth grade when I got to Granny's. I had never been to school before."

"I didn't know that."

She tossed her tissue on the floor, "I've told you this."

He shook his head, "I would have remembered."

"Well, I don't want to talk about it anymore."

"You always shut me out, Angeline,"

"I said-"

"-Angeline."

"-Cricket!"

"-I know, I know."

Angeline was a blur as she disappeared out the door.

He stood in the doorway watching her walk across the field. He turned suddenly and trudged back inside, shaking his head.

Cricket sat at the table, fuming. He grabbed the newspaper and waited for her return.

Cricket heard the door bang 15 minutes later. He looked up quickly and back down again. He rattled his paper.

Angeline sat down at the table. She picked up a piece of bread from the plate he had fixed for her and began to eat. The storm had passed.

Cricket noticed her picking at her food.

"Tell me about the Barter Faire," he made an attempt at conversation.

"I met a really sweet woman. Her name is Magpie. She drives a bus with a beautiful blue and yellow mural painted on the outside." He remembered seeing that bus, and the weirdos that had come from the bus into the store. Good grief.

"What was that face?" she said suddenly.

"Nothing, keep going."

"So anyway, I was able to set up my table and - Oh! I have a box of stuff to show you!" She ran outside to get it from the backseat.

26

Angeline's barter box

When she got back into the house, she plopped her box of treasures down onto the floor of the kitchen with a big smile.

"Check this out!" Angeline began to take things from the box and hold them up to show her husband.

"Two dresses, a clock, a mirror…" she began as she took them out and set them on the table.

"-some tomatoes, a wooden box, and a necklace and earring set…"

He watched skeptically.

"…and here's that garlic you asked for."

"Is this the trend, now? I mean did you get any money or just 'magic beans', Jack?"

Her chin went down and her eyebrows went up, not a good sign.

"You are talking to me about bringing in money? When was the last time you contributed to the household?"

Cricket pointed his finger at her.

"Well, you spent all day in Fairy Land when we were supposed to be having a vacation together." He reminded her.

"Spending time together. Remember?"

"FAIRY LAND?" She raged back at him and threw the garlic back into the box.

"I was having a good time; I met some great people, for once. It's always about YOU, today was about ME!"

Cricket's head shrugged down into his shoulders. "What do you mean it's always about ME? Why do you say that? You've never said that before."

Angeline turned away from him.

"You wouldn't understand."

"I would understand," Cricket had lowered his voice, "tell me what you're trying to say."

Angeline looked back at him and pulled a chair from the table and sat. The table that held all her treasures that she had been so happy with a few minutes ago.

"You don't know what it was like for me when I was growing up. We were squatters. We lived in a tree house, for God's sake."

"What was that like?"

"It feels shameful."

"Where was it?"

"Near a place called Chicken Creek in Nevada. I'm not sure where exactly."

"What did you do all day?"

"My mom home-schooled me and I did a lot of exploring.

"You've never been back there?"

"No."

27

Scorpio and Magpie

The sunset was beautiful in July. Not many people were in the mood for sleep. Even the babies were up late when the music began in earnest. The separate camps each had their own unique group of musicians. They all played and talked and laughed for hours into the night. Starry Night camp had the oldtime fiddlers. People wandered by, they stopped to listen and began to dance to the old tunes played on fiddle, guitar and mandolin. A tenor guitar player from another camp joined in. Magpie played the fiddle with flair. She had won awards at the National Fiddle competition in years past. Magpie could play for hours and never repeat a song.

"Oh bury me beneath the willow
Under the weeping willow tree
So she will know where I am sleeping
And perhaps she'll weep for me."

Magpie sang the chorus and then commenced to saw the fiddle with the bow while the other musicians backed her up.

Scorpio sat in the shadows, preferring it to the light of the bonfire. He watched for Angeline. He hadn't seen her all evening. She said she'd be back tomorrow anyway. Scorpio had a change of clothes that he had picked up that day from some guy who had a real live barn owl at his booth.

Scorpio had enough food to tide him over and a place to sleep on the bus tonight. He had slept most of the last 5 years away, so he wasn't in any hurry to turn in tonight.

Magpie came and sat for a few moments next to Scorpio, she was eating from a bag of popcorn.

"So where you from?" she asked him.

"Walla Walla."

"I picked you up in Pendleton."

"I know."

"You had some luck hitching a ride that far."

"I was on a farm truck."

"So how'd you fall off a ladder?"

"Actually, I fell off the truck."

She thought about this and crunched her popcorn; her fingers were yellow with brewers yeast.

"So who are you, really? I know you've got a better story than the one you're telling."

Her big purple Mexican blouse floated around her breasts and down to her waist; the multicolored skirt was blooming about her hips. She had taken off the headscarf sometime during the day and her dark hair was loose and messy down to her shoulder blades.

"I escaped from Walla Walla prison during the earthquake."

"Ha! I could feel the aura of secrecy around you, Scorpio. I feel like you're telling me the truth now," she laughed.

Why did no one care that he had escaped from prison?

"So, what do you think about me now?" he asked her from the shadows.

She stared at his face for a moment and answered, "I think you are capable of change."

"You don't even know what I did."

"Doesn't matter."

"What if I killed someone?"

"I don't think you did," she quipped.

He laughed at her, "I didn't."

"The thing is, Scorpio, what are you going to do from now on?"

"I am going to run my own damn life for a change."

"Sounds like a good start."

"I'm going to start smoking."

"Well, okay then."

"There you go, smirking again."

"Honey, I admire the fact that you found a way to get yourself out and you are trying to grasp ahold of a better life. Even if that life includes cigarettes."

"So what do you do in your real life?" he asked her.

"This is my real life."

"You ride around in a bus and go to Fairy pageants?"

"'Don't underestimate the value of doing nothing.'"

"Is that a quote?"

"Ever heard of Piglet?"

"You live your life according to a children's book?"

"You should try it."

"If a man has two pennies he should buy a loaf of bread with one to sustain his life, and a flower with the other to give him a reason to live," Scorpio quoted.

"Where'd you get that from?" she asked.

"It's in the bible."

"That's not from the bible."

"It's in Proverbs."

Her dimples flashed as she laughed, "It is not."

He sat forward, "Ever heard of The Language of Insects?"

"I've heard of it," Magpie replied.

"This guy says that insects have meaning, symbolic of your character. You were right on when you defined Scorpio."

"Angeline was talking about that book this morning."

He asked about Angeline. "She told me she's coming back tomorrow."

"She'll do some more tattoos. Are you going to get one?"

"I might."

"What do you have now?"

"A black widow spider, a Scorpion, a full back piece of an eagle."

"Are they prison tattoos?"

"Just the spider."

Magpie picked up her fiddle again; the guys were calling her back to the bonfire.

"You can sleep in the bus if you want," she told him,

Magpie wiped her hands and grabbed her fiddle as she went to join the others.

Scorpio watched as she walked away.

28

Breakfast alone

Angeline and Cricket went to bed early. Angeline was exhausted from the day and Cricket wanted to lie beside her even though he wasn't tired. He reached out for her to see if she was receptive to him. She wasn't. Angeline only wanted him to hold her until she fell asleep.

Angeline was the first one up in the morning, Cricket could smell coffee coming from the kitchen.

"Angeline," he called from the bedroom.

"It's almost ready," she called back.

Angeline brought two cups to the bed and slipped beneath the covers with him. Then handed him his cup.

"I thought we could go for a hike to Blue Lake."

"Sorry, I'm going back to the Barter Faire today."

"Angeline! What about spending time with me?"

"Oh. My. God. Grow up!" Angeline got out of bed and took her cup out to the kitchen table. It was such a small cabin; there was only the kitchen with a table, the bedroom and a small bathroom with a shower. There wasn't really anywhere else to go.

"Grow up? Me? YOU grow up!"

"You're going to spend the day trading goofy-ass trinkets for tattoos when you should be charging good money. We are losing money every day that you don't work."

"Um, hey, why am I the one that is supporting us?" Angeline fumed at him.

"I thought you believed in me." Cricket hollered from the bed, "I thought you believed in my book."

"I do! But you could get out there and make money, too. Selling your book doesn't take all day long every day."

Angeline took her cup to the sink and poured out her coffee.

"If you want me to get groceries today, you need to leave me some money, by the way," Cricket added.

"God, Cricket, I gave you $100 yesterday. What happened to that?"

Before he could respond, Angeline stuck her head through the bedroom doorway.

"I'm leaving now. I'm sure you can figure out how to take care of yourself for one day."

Cricket went to a little hole in the wall café for breakfast that morning. He had enough money for breakfast anyway, and he didn't feel like cooking after the way she slammed out of the cabin this morning. Why in the world would anyone want to go spend the day with hundreds of unwashed hippies and their worthless objects?

He could go hiking alone. From the guidebook he found in the cabin, Blue Lake looked like it would be a 2-hour hike. He would pick up a lunch from the Pub and take it with him. He packed the camera and dressed in layers, even though it was July. The book mentioned there could be snow up there. At the last minute he grabbed two bottles of water and some matches. What else? His little collection boxes. He might find some new species in the Northwest that he could gather.

The waitress came up to his table. "Everything okay here?" she asked.

"Have you been to Blue Lake?"

"Lots of times."

"How long does it take to get there?"

"About two hours."

"Is it a pretty easy hike?"

"Well, me and my grandma did it last year. So, yeah."

He stacked his silverware on his plate and he drained the last of his coffee.

"Guess I'm on my way, then," Cricket dropped his money on the table and left.

29

Cricket & Brad hike to Blue Lake

Cricket ran into Brad outside the Hoot Owl. It was the local 'breakfast only' hole in the wall.

"So she's at the Fairy thing again today," he told Brad.

"Well, what are you doing today, then?"

"We were going hiking to Blue Lake, I guess I'll go by myself. Have you been there before?"

"Yep. Last summer I went up there. Beautiful place, there's gray jays there that'll eat out of your hand. I've got pictures of a bird eating a cracker off the top of my head."

Brad got his cell phone from his pocket and showed Cricket the picture.

"Well, you want to come hiking with me?"

"Sure, I guess so, why not?"

They walked to Brad's truck together and Cricket followed him to his ranch so he could change his clothes and get his pack.

"We can ride together in my pickup," Brad said. Cricket left the car at Brad's place and they took off for the lake.

"Did you grow up back east?" Brad asked him as they drove up the highway.

"My folks are from the Northwest, actually. They moved to Delaware when I was a child. What about you?"

"Colorado. When I was a teenager we moved to California. That was quite an experience, growing up in the 60s in California."

"I'll bet. How did you end up here?"

"I was commissioned to paint a mural and I ended up staying."

"Is that what you do, paint murals?"

"I paint signs, I've done all the business signs you see for this town. Everyone seems to like my work."

"So how did you come up with the fiddle contest and the Giant Insect Contest? Do you play fiddle?"

"I play everything except the fiddle, actually. But I love to hang out with musicians. I love to bring this unique American Folk Art to the general public. These are some of the best people you'll ever get to know."

Cricket could tell Brad was passionate about his contest. "Well, I can't wait to see how this works."

They were at the turnoff to the trail that went to Blue Lake. The truck slowed down, made the turn and they parked in the lot.

"I haven't been here in a long time; this is going to be great!" Brad was enthusiastic as they got out of the truck and retrieved their packs.

The day was sunny and hot. They made sure they had plenty of water. Brad found a bag of bread for the birds. Cricket brought his camera and they both had snacks. This was turning out to be a good day after all, he thought. Brad knew all about the geology of the area and the history. He said there were fossils nearby so he had his rock hammer ready to do some collecting.

"Angeline would love this," Cricket commented on their way up the trail.

"Well, I guess she's missing out."

30

Tick comes to town asking questions

The bartender came to the back office where Andrew was counting slips from the previous night. Andrew had his elbow on the desk, and was massaging his forehead with his right hand as he stared at the adding machine. Numbers didn't come easy to him, but who else would do this if he didn't?

"There's a guy here says he needs to talk to you."

"Right now? I can't stop what I'm doing." Andrew looked up at Patrick and saw a man standing behind him. The man looked like an undercover cop with that black suit.

"He says it's important," Patrick stepped aside and black-suit stood in the doorway.

Andrew searched his brain for what kind of trouble he could be in. *Shit.*

"Come on in," he stood and hoped that this wasn't an IRS agent. He felt his face flush at the thought.

Black-suit held out his card, "Name's Tim Blick. You can call me Tick."

"Tick," they shook hands and the guy sat down.

Andrew looked at his card, an investigator for the US Marshal's Office. *Oh Hell.*

This guy looked like a bald Hulk Hogan. In a suit. He could jump right over the desk and do a leg drop on Andrew and –

Tick was holding out a photo for Andrew to take.

"Who's this?" he asked the Marshal.

"I guess that means you haven't seen this guy?"

"No."

It was an intake shot of a guy with dirty blond hair. He looked pretty average.

"Here's my card. Call me if you see him."

"Does he have a name?"

"Scorpio."

The Hulk left before Andrew could ask any more questions. That was weird.

"What did Hulk want?" Patrick was standing at the door to Andrew's office.

"He's looking for some guy."

"Does he think this guy is in Utopia?"

He waved his hand for Patrick to leave, "I don't know. I gotta get these taxes done."

31

Memories of Blue Lake

Scorpio woke Saturday morning on one of the converted bus seats. This was the best bed he'd slept in for the past five years. He could smell campfires and bacon; which made him think of when he was a kid camping and fishing with his dad.

"Are we going to Blue Lake today, Dad?"

Scorpio had jumped out of bed as soon as the sun came up and had all his stuff packed from the night before. He was standing in the kitchen, watching his pops pouring coffee.

"Soon as we get the car loaded."

Jump jump, skip skip, run around the kitchen.

"Hey hey hey! You're going to wake up your mother."

"What kind of fish will we get again, dad?"

"Lake trout, little bug," his dad always called him that. His real name was Ray, but he changed his name to Scorpio after reading the best comic book ever and insisted everyone call him by his new name.

Lying on the bus seat, he noticed the ceiling, *Christ, there was even a psychedelic painting up there.*

When he was 13, he didn't want to go with his pops anymore. It was more fun hanging with the guys. There were four of them. They had met in Middle School. They were compadres, amigos, even though Rocco was the only Mexican. Rocco was also the instigator. Scorpio's mom tried to warn him about Rocco, but all the guys looked up to him. Rocco was fearless. He had a tattoo gun that he got on the Internet, which is how Scorpio got his first tattoo. A Scorpion on his upper arm; it was as big as the pistol Rocco had in his coat pocket when they went into the liquor store that day.

Scorpio was searching for some sticks to throw in the fire when he saw Angeline drive by looking for a place to park. She didn't see him, but he saw her. *Oh, I am going to get me some of that.* The anticipation was driving him wild. This was the kind of woman he dreamed about in prison.

Today Magpie was wearing a long dress of sky blue fabric that was covered with outlines of white herons. Her hair was in one braid down her back with tendrils already springing out around her face. She was big and she was beautiful, lush and soft. When you hugged Magpie it was like falling into a vat of peaches.

She was looking forward to seeing her new friend again. There was an instant connection between them; they had so much to talk about. She was also happy with her new tattoo. She looked at it again and decided it needed more lotion.

Scorpio got a paper plate, grabbed a fork and helped himself to what was in the pan. Life didn't get better than this.

"She's here, you know." Scorpio mentioned.

Magpie looked up at him from rummaging in her pack.

"I saw her drive by when I went to get wood," he continued.

Magpie stood up and saw Angeline stepping across the grass toward their camp. Angeline's brown hair was carelessly gathered with a ribbon that flowed down her back. Her toenails showed pink through her sandals. Her smile was contagious as she approached the camp and saw Magpie.

The white embroidered sundress she wore showed just enough cleavage to set Scorpio's imagination on fire.

Magpie waved her over, "Hey! We were just talking about you. Come and have some breakfast."

Angeline was happy to see Magpie but didn't really want to hang out with Scorpio. She entered the camp and set down her suitcase.

32

Scorpio trades his dog for a tattoo

Scorpio watched as Angeline and Magpie talked near the fire. He needed to have his ribs wrapped again but his ankle wasn't hurting so bad. Scorpio thought Magpie might give him another pill. He had searched the bus but hadn't been able to find them anywhere.

"Magpie," he called to her. She looked up from her breakfast conversation.

"Can I get another pill from you? I mean if it's not too much bother. My ribs are really hurting me this morning."

"Honey, you only get one. I know you're not hurt that badly."

"Well, can you wrap my ribs again? It's all come loose."

"You can take care of yourself now, Scorpio. I can tell when you are looking for attention."

God, what was it with this woman? Could she read his mind? Maybe she knew what his intentions were with Angeline. He looked at her a little more closely.

"What's wrong?" Angeline actually looked at him. His heart throbbed when she met his eyes. Oh Jeez, her eyes were stunning. And her hair. He wanted to untie her hair and run his hands through it.

He wasn't answering, so Magpie filled her in.

"He bruised his ribs and had a twisted ankle when I picked him up."

"I fell off a ladder," he finished when he could speak.

Angeline noticed him looking at her breasts when he was talking. *She had always hated that. God!*

He looked at her face again and tried to clear his mind.

"Can you do a tattoo for me today?" he asked.

Angeline didn't want to, "What are you thinking of?"

"Can I look at your album?" She opened her suitcase and pulled out the portfolio.

Angeline walked over to Scorpio and opened it for him to look at. What else could she do? She had to be polite.

Angeline turned around and went back to the fire right away, feeling safer next to Magpie.

"Oh wait! Hey! I recognize this, do you have that book?"

"What book?"

"*The Language of Insects*."

She laughed, "My husband wrote that book."

My husband, well, things just got more exciting.

"I have a copy of that book, I mean, I did."

"So what do you want?"

I want you.

"A silverfish."

She felt the blood rush from her head. Why would he choose that?

Magpie commented, "Hungry soul."

"Can you put it on my inner thigh?" It was worth a try.

Angeline recoiled, but hid it well. Her philosophy was such that she would tattoo anyone where they wanted it. Could she pull this off?

"Scorpio, what are you up to?" Magpie called him out.

"What? I've always wanted a tattoo there, if she's good, it won't hurt. Anyway, it'll keep my mind off the pain in my ribs. It really hurts to breathe."

"I bet," Magpie said.

Scorpio was looking at Angeline again, waiting for an answer.

She wasn't ready to set up the table yet.

"I don't feel like leaving the camp right now."

"Then you can do me right here." *Double entendre.*

Magpie lifted her eyebrows; she caught it. Angeline pretended she didn't. She still hadn't decided to give him a tattoo anyway.

"What have you got to trade me? I'm not doing tattoos for free."

"I've got a dog."

Both women looked at Juno who was sleeping under the bus.

"What? She's a stray. She followed me when I was hitchhiking, I've only had her a few weeks."

"I can't take your dog." But she was thinking about it.

"I don't have a job right now, how can I feed her?"

Juno looked up at them from under the bus as if she knew they were talking about her.

"You can't feed her?"

"No."

Angeline was thinking; she looked at Magpie who made an 'I'm staying out of this' gesture.

She felt sorry for the dog.

"Okay, I'll take her."

Just like that.

He perked up, "You will?"

She walked over to the bus and crouched down.

"Come here, Juno, come here sweetie." She held out her hand. The dog's whole body began wiggling and her head nodded around like a horse and she sneezed twice in a row. Then she got up and nuzzled Angeline who threw her arm around her as she sat down. They sat like that for a while. Angeline stood up and Juno crawled back under the bus to lie in the cool shade.

"I said, I'll take her," she conceded, unpacking her stuff.

33

Scorpio's tattoo

Scorpio became aroused thinking about Angeline and his new tattoo. He imagined her soft hands touching his inner thigh and her face close, her hair tickling his leg. She might get carried away and ...

"Hello? Scorpio? I said how big do you want this tattoo?"

"About seven inches"

"You're not funny," said Magpie.

"What?" He looked up at the girls and smiled.

"Okay, about this big," he indicated with his fingers.

Angeline set up the area as best she could and then with a look at Magpie that said, 'don't leave me' she commenced to sterilize the area.

She was wiping his inner thigh with alcohol and Scorpio was watching her. Angeline tried to make this as clinical as possible, which was not working out for her. She saw that he was getting off on this but she didn't know what to do. How did she get into this predicament?

Angeline looked over at Juno and kept going. Scorpio arrogantly spread his legs wider. When Angeline clicked the switch on the gun, it began to buzz and she concentrated on the task at hand. There was no ignoring his arousal. The more she focused on her work, the more distracted she got. Scorpio wasn't moaning, but he might as well have been. Then, without intention, she began to feel something. His desire was contagious. She felt the familiar wetness and then an ache that became stronger as she worked on the design. She hated this guy. He was rude and inappropriate. That was the word, inappropriate.

There was something about him that didn't fit in with everyone else. Nonetheless, here she was, and the waves of lust that were radiating from him felt like the tide dragging her in. She tried to focus more on her work.

Scorpio watched intently while Angeline sat between his legs. *Oh, baby.* As she applied the needle to his soft skin, he wanted to reach out his hands and put one on each side of her head.

Angeline was feeling a trembling in her stomach as she silently etched the legs of the silverfish on his skin. Her graceful hands were damp with sweat but she thought she better just keep going and get this over with. How could she explain the way her body was reacting to him? She couldn't.

Finally, Angeline finished the last detail. Scorpio watched intently as she smoothed Vaseline on his leg, he could barely stand it. She put a square of plastic on the area and secured it with tape. Then she stood up and pulled the needle from the gun, took off her gloves and put everything into a plastic baggie to throw away. Throwing everything into the suitcase, she shut the lid a little harder than she meant to. Her face was hot and her whole body felt damp. Neither of them had spoken yet, there was an awkward silence.

"Would you like some coffee?" Magpie asked.

"I need to go," Angeline answered. "I'll leave Juno where she is until I'm done for the day, is that okay?" She looked at Magpie.

"Of course."

Scorpio watched her walk away and knew he would eventually get just what he wanted. He headed for the bus for a private moment by himself.

34

New friends

Angeline was still shook up when she arrived at the tent where she had her table the day before. Curious customers watched as she set up her equipment, they began to gather and look at her pamphlets and artwork.

"Cool, I want an Egyptian Beetle!" Someone was ready for a tattoo.

"Who's first?" Angeline smiled and tried to distract herself from what had just happened at the camp.

Angeline had her box beside her and it began to fill with goodies she didn't even know she wanted until she saw them: a hand painted silk scarf, a bag of tomatoes, jars of relish, pickles and jam.

Angeline was thinking about the argument she and Cricket had this morning. They argued all the time, and she was really tired of it. She kept thinking it was just a phase, but it never passed. That's another reason why she didn't want to hang around with him all day. He was so hard on people; critical of everyone. No one could do anything right the way he saw it. Especially her.

Angeline was thinking that she needed to relax, but she wanted to avoid the yoga tent after yesterday. She didn't like it when her memories crowded in on her with no warning. Maybe a massage would be a better idea. There were plenty of opportunities here for a massage. Maybe one of them would trade?

She had done about four tattoos and needed a break.

"Come back later, guys, I need to find some food," Angeline said to the group that was waiting.

Packing her suitcase, she carried it with her to the grill a few steps away. There was a picnic table where she sat and ate and listened to the music playing nearby.

"Hey Angel," Magpie said.

She looked up, "Have a seat," she invited.

Magpie sat at the picnic table across from Angeline and began to unwrap her sandwich.

"Well, you are having an experience," Magpie began.

"You could say that again," Angeline replied.

"What the hell was that about this morning?"

"I know, right?"

Angeline was shaking her head and picking at her food.

"How well do you know Scorpio?" Angeline asked her friend.

"I just met him when I picked him up hitching a ride."

"There's something wrong with him."

"He's been in prison the last five years."

"That explains a lot."

They ate and watched the people around them.

"Hey, Magpie!" A young couple with a baby came up to the table and joined them. Magpie introduced them to Angeline and they all visited while they ate lunch.

"Cameron and Kristin live in Utopia. You'll probably see them around if you stay here long enough."

It made her happy to meet the locals; she was enjoying herself despite the few weird things that had happened.

"Hey, do you know who would trade a massage for a tattoo?" she remembered to ask.

"Oh, say, come with me, I'll take you to a friend of mine," Kristin invited.

"Do you want to come along?" Angeline asked Magpie.

"No, I've got to work at the booth for a little bit, I'll see you later."

The girls took off down the path.

"Are you moving to Utopia?" Kristin asked Angeline.

"My husband and I are visiting. He's going to judge the Giant Insect Contest next month. I wouldn't mind living here, though."

"Oh cool, we go to the contest every year." She readjusted the baby sling while they walked.

"Where's your husband? Does he have a booth here, too?"

"He wouldn't come with me. He would hate this."

"I'm sorry," Kristin said.

"God, he has been so hard to get along with lately. We can't stop fighting."

Kristin stopped and looked at Angeline while the crowd moved around them.

"I know what that feels like. You must be very frustrated." She had focused her whole attention on Angeline and it seemed so intimate all of a sudden.

"I'm dealing with enough of my own shit. I don't need this."

"I know. It can be overwhelming." Kristin nursed her baby while they talked.

"Maybe being here for a day or two will give you both a break.

"Maybe." Angeline said doubtfully, "But this began before we even got to Utopia."

"Can you talk to someone about this?"

"I don't know who. I'm always the one trying to keep the peace," Angeline divulged.

Kristin set her hand on Angeline's arm, "It sounds like you are in a time of transition. That's not always easy."

"You're right."

They continued to talk and Angeline was so grateful to be able to discuss her frustrations about Cricket with someone. It had been a long time since she could talk to anybody.

Soon they made their way to the massage space. It was a booth set up with a soft table, sweet music and beautiful scarves hanging all around the tent, they were swaying in the breeze.

"This is Tamar," said Kristin.

"Tamar, this is Angeline, can you trade with her?"

"What do you have, Angeline?"

"I do tattoos."

"I would love that! I'm in."

35

In which we find Tick making a plan

Timothy Blick loved his job. He had a passion for justice. He wanted to get the bad guy. Blick was righteous, stubborn, and as fearless as a superhero. He shaved his head to look severe, intimidating. Did his facial hair like the Hulk on purpose. Knew how to wrestle. When Tim Blick started martial arts as a young boy, he had every intention of chasing bad guys some day.

Tick. It just fit him.

Now he was after Scorpio, and he knew the scumbag had to be close by. The guy had escaped from Walla Walla during the earthquake. They were lucky he was the only one. It took them a few hours to figure out who was missing with all the chaos.

When they did, they called Tick. He had a reputation as being indefatigable, and he wouldn't stop until Scorpio was in custody. The con had 10 more years to do. It was just a hunch that brought the officer to this area.

He was staying in a hotel, showing the inmate's photo around.

He woke that morning to the whirring of the air conditioner; it was going to be a hot day in Utopia. Tick made hotel coffee in the mini pot that sat on the bathroom counter. He was a little repulsed by the idea of making coffee in the bathroom and decided he would move the unit to the bedside table tomorrow morning. He sat on the plaid upholstered chair by the window and looked at the stack of papers in his lap. Maybe he would change hotels. There wasn't even a tiny table and chair, and it smelled like mildew in here. He would make the call after he finished his paperwork.

Speaking of making a call, Tick had to make a courtesy call to the Sheriff this morning. Let him know he was in the area, let him know about the assignment that was given to him by his supervisor. Tick added that to the list.

Tick needed a plan of attack to catch Scorpio. He could feel the presence of this inmate, this reprobate, degenerate troublemaker. Scorpio probably wasn't dangerous, but he was flaunting the law simply by being free. All lawbreakers belonged in prison.

This agent only had ten more days before they would put him on another assignment, so he had to use all his focus to capture Scorpio before his time was up. Tick rarely lost a man.

How far should he go for this mission? He began his list.

Set up roadblocks? This was a prison escapee, after all. This didn't seem the right tactic in this case, but it went on his list.

Check all bars and restaurants, then grocery stores. In some cases you don't want the offender to know you are on his trail, but in this case, it seemed the right thing to do. That went on his list.

Background research, Tick had done his homework on that subject. Scorpio's real name was Raymond Monroe. Born in Silverdale Washington. Age 26. Crime, accessory to armed robbery. His reputation and behavior while in Walla Walla was exemplary. He probably would have been out on parole within the year. Guess he didn't know or didn't care. Could anyone be so lucky as to have an earthquake open up your cell wall?

Tick had been to Silverdale and spent part of his two-week assignment doing research there, and all fingers pointed to Utopia.

He had heard of a Barter Faire going on at the fairgrounds five miles down the road. That was one of the places he was going to research today. Tick was sure he could make some headway at the freak show. Before he got ready to head down there, he thought he'd take a quick trip to Blue Lake. Raymond and his dad used to go fishing and camping there. Tick had interviewed a cousin while he was in Silverdale last week.

"Scorpio and his dad went on a trip every year to Blue Lake, down by Utopia," he said, "those were the happiest times of his life." That was the statement that Tick had focused on throughout the interview.

He showered and changed into his flannel shirt, jeans and tennis shoes, then grabbed a bottle of water and his new backpack and headed for the car. Tick hoped the trail wasn't too hard. He didn't have hiking boots. Before he left town for the lake, he stopped at Harvest Foods to pick up some juice and almonds for breakfast, and a sub sandwich from the deli for lunch. He took his handful of vitamins with juice back at the car and then went in search of Blue Lake.

36

Cricket & Brad are hiking and see a guy

"What a beautiful area you live in. I have half a mind to move here," Cricket remarked. They walked down the packed dirt trail, one following the other. Cricket was really looking forward to finding some indigenous insects while they were out today. Brad had a passion for insects, too, so they spent a lot of time inspecting trees and flowers and shrubs as they walked along.

They passed by a creek and cupped their hands to catch water to cool off. It was so hot. Brad took off his hat and soaked it in the stream and put it on his head. Cricket did the same with his t-shirt.

By the time they got to the lake, they were really hungry and broke out the sandwiches and granola bars. The gray jays watched from the treetops as the men unpacked their lunches. Brad showed Cricket how the birds would swoop down and eat from his hand. The birds seemed tame as they flew from the top of the cedar tree, grabbed the food and then flew back up.

Mostly, they just hung around talking. Cricket hadn't had anyone to talk to for so long, and neither had Brad. They were really enjoying the day.

Tick was walking up the trail looking around for signs of anyone camping or living in the area, in case this was where Raymond was hanging out. He heard voices of people coming down the trail and saw two men in t-shirts and tennis shoes. He greeted them as they came near.

"Good afternoon," he nodded to them.

"Hey there."

"Hot day."

Tick stopped in the trail, so they waited to see what he wanted.

"I'm looking for a man who might be up here. Have you seen anyone? He has blond hair, green eyes, and is 5'9'. He has a tattoo of a scorpion on his upper arm. Here's a picture."

"There's no one up at the lake right now," said Brad.

"Who is this guy?" asked Cricket. They looked at the picture.

"His name is Scorpio and I need to talk to him."

They stood for a minute waiting for details, but Tick kept them to himself.

"Well, okay then, we'll let you know if we see anyone like that."

Tick handed them his card and continued up the trail.

They didn't talk until they were out of hearing range and then Brad elbowed Cricket.

"Think that guy is a fugitive or something?"

"Well, this one looked like a US Marshal, so I would guess so, yeah. Didn't he look like that famous wrestler?"

"Anyway, who hikes through the forest in July with a flannel shirt?"

"Did you see his pack? It looks like LL Bean extravaganza. For a day hike?"

They laughed.

"You'd think we would have heard something on the news."

"I know."

They got to the car and drove down the road, listening to Cat Stevens.

37

Tick at the Barter Faire

Tick didn't have any luck at Blue Lake, but he had to try everything. It was a great place, but he had wasted his time. It was about 3:00 when he got back to the parking lot and took off for the Barter Faire. It shouldn't take him more than 30 minutes to get there. Tick knew people would notice him in this getup, but he would look even scarier in tie-dye, so he decided to change into biker gear at the hotel first. Tick looked natural in leather with a Harley rag tied on his head. He even had the boots.

When he got to the gate, it was crazy. The costumes these people were wearing were amazing. The hairstyles were outrageous. The various outfits and the things they were carrying were interesting.

He saw a man dressed in black pants and suspenders; his facial hair consisted of a beard without a mustache. He looked like a Mennonite, except for the reticulated python draped across the back of his neck and down his arm. It was yellow and brown like a tiger.

Another was playing a concertina, and singing. One was walking on stilts and dressed like a giant peacock. This was going to be an interesting afternoon.

Tick decided to keep the picture and questions to himself. He would notice the guy if he saw him. He had memorized his picture. Now it was just a matter of walking around and looking. There were picnic tables up and down the grass corridor that was formed by the booths lined up on either side. He sat at one of the tables and observed for a little while.

"Would you like to buy some flowers?" A young teen approached him with a bucket full of bouquets.

"No thanks," Tick grunted.

"You could take them to your girlfriend. Everyone likes flowers."

Tick ignored her and she walked on. He kept watching. This guy would definitely have short hair. He was a scrawny kind of guy, wiry and sneaky. Tick would love to run into him. He would grab him by the back of both his arms and twist them behind him and push him to the front gate. He would throw him in the car and take the triumphant drive back to the local police station and make his calls from there.

Tick rose from the picnic table and walked among the crowd.

He looked for the hiding places where the pot smokers hang out. Scorpio wouldn't be out in the daylight. This guy was going to be hiding out. The woods were dank when he entered from the creek side. There were circles of people hanging out and smoking pot, talking and sitting on stumps. They were laughing and having a good time. He couldn't be too obvious, but he tried to search the faces of the guys who looked close to the perp's description.

"Wanna burn one?" A guy dressed like a pirate looked at him and handed him a joint.

"No thanks. I'm looking for Scorpio."

"Ain't seen him, man."

Tick continued walking through the cedars, crushing the soft fragrant needles beneath his feet. He could hear and feel the beat of the drum circle from across the river. He came out onto one of the camp meadows where there were buses as far as the eye could see. Many were custom painted by various levels of artists. Tick decided to walk around the camps and take a look. His instinct told him that Raymond was here.

38

Scorpio sees Tick through the bus window

Scorpio lay on his makeshift bed in the bus. He was one satisfied man. Getting the tattoo was a good idea, he just thought of it off the cuff. Angeline felt something for him. He could almost smell her desire while she worked on him. It wasn't going to take long to get what he wanted.

He got up and looked through the food boxes in the bus and grabbed some apples. That would do for now. Was there any more cash around here? Where was Magpie's pharmacy? He looked out the window as he searched, making sure no one caught him.

He froze in his tracks and ducked down. His blood ran so cold he got goose bumps. Jesus Joseph and Mary, that was a freakin' cop. He knew it was; he could spot one from 50 yards. He had lived with them 24/7 these last 5 years. *Holy Shit.* His mind was spinning.

Crouching until he thought it was safe to look through the bus window, Scorpio barely peeked out and saw the guy's back to him. The cop was in Harley gear, but that didn't fool him. This cop was looking for him. It wasn't his paranoia talking; the cop was after him. How had this cop found him? Oh shit, Magpie and Angeline were coming with another girl who was carrying a baby. The cop stopped and talked to them, then Scorpio saw them all turn to look at the bus. He ducked down again. How was he going to get out of this predicament?

39

Tick talks to the women in the camp

"We stay in that bus," Magpie pointed and they all looked at the bus when the Harley guy asked where they were camped.

"I live in Utopia, I'm not camped here," answered a young mother with her baby in a sling.

"Well, I was just wondering. I'm looking for an old friend of mine and he said he might be here this weekend."

"I know some people here," said Magpie. "I've been coming here for a few years." She was hesitant, something felt phony about this guy. She had a sense about things and she always listened to what her impressions told her.

"His name is Scorpio."

"- Hey, Magpie" Angeline started.

"- I don't know anyone named Scorpio. What does he look like?" Magpie asked.

Tick didn't want to show them the mug shot, who has a mug shot of their friend?

"Blond guy, green eyes. Scorpion tattooed on his arm."

Silverfish on his inner thigh thought Angeline.

They were shaking their heads. "I'll let you know if we run into him," Magpie said.

Tick knew he was here somewhere.

40

We won't turn you in

"Juno, sweetie, what a good girl," Angeline squatted and held out her hand. Juno came over, waiting for a good scratching. She was a mellow dog so they didn't tie her up; she just hung around without running off.

"Cool dog," commented Kristin.

"She really is," said Angeline.

"You can come out now," said Magpie.

Angeline and Kristin looked at Magpie, what was she talking about?

Scorpio stood up and stretched like he had been napping and came down the aisle of the bus and down the stairs.

"What?" he said.

Angeline felt her palms grow damp all of a sudden.

Kristin looked at the man who had just come off the bus and then at Magpie and Angeline. She raised her eyebrows and Magpie nodded.

"So, looks like you got a new friend," Magpie goaded.

"Yeah, right." He wasn't amused. Would they turn him in?

"You're safe here, honey. We have a philosophy: 'Live and let live'. You make your own life; I won't interfere. Whatever you've done, just live your own life as best you can."

Magpie flashed her dimples and laughed. "I don't judge anyone, it's all good."

What kind of a place is this where he wouldn't get turned in? He had escaped from prison for God sakes. Utopia was a fitting name for this town.

Meanwhile, Angeline was noticing the way Scorpio was leaning on the side of the bus. He was absently running his fingers up and down his jaw, thinking about something. His eyes green like the sea. He caught her looking at him and winked. How could she be repulsed by someone and attracted at the same time? Her heart was confused, that's all.

She squatted by Juno *it was time to go home.*

"I guess I'll take my dog and go home. I've been gone two days now; I'm sure my husband will be glad to see me," Angeline said uncertainly. She patted her leg and called the dog who followed with a cheerful bounce.

"Okay, will we see you tonight?" asked Magpie. "This is the night of the Fairy Congress, you can't miss that."

"Maybe," Angeline answered. She wanted to see whatever that was, but more than that, she wanted to see Scorpio again.

Angeline felt her face flush as she walked away. *What was going on with her*? "Come on, Juno, good girl" She slapped her leg and reached out to pat the dog as they made their way to the parking lot. Angeline tried to concentrate on Cricket, how he loved her, the way his eyes crinkled when he smiled. They might be going through a rough patch right now. But they would get through it.

Angeline was walking the grassy path to the car when she heard Scorpio's voice behind her.

"What about you, Angeline, would you turn me in?"

She turned toward Scorpio's voice and smoothed her hands down her skirt, then set them on her hips.

"Why would I do that," she answered. "You've never done anything to me."

Scorpio nodded, then knelt down and caressed Juno's head. When he looked up at Angeline she was watching his hand like a sparrow hypnotized by a cobra.

"Listen, Angeline, when are you coming back?"

She crossed her arms and shifted her body. *Was she coming back?*

She heard a buzzing in her head, her face felt hot. Those eyes, and his reckless attitude toward life. He acted like nothing mattered.

Angeline folded her hands together in front of her in an effort to stop them from trembling.

He stood up.

"So, what do you want, Angeline?" Scorpio asked and stepped closer.

"What do you mean?" She asked.

Slowly, he reached out for her hand, never dropping his gaze from her face.

"Angeline," his voice was low and intimate.

She looked at him.

"What do you want," he repeated softly.

Scorpio reached out his hand and gently ran his fingertip along her jaw. She felt it burn her skin and she looked away from him.

He stepped closer and softly pressed his forehead against hers.

"Angeline," her name was poetry.

She shrugged her shoulders and shook her head slowly.

"I don't know," she whispered.

His hand slid to the back of her neck, his fingers gently tangled in her hair. Scorpio made her look at him.

Angeline's gaze never wavered as he brought his face closer and brushed her lips with his. His fingers tightened on her hair as he kissed her harder. His other hand reached around her body and pressed her closer to him.

She stiffened and pushed at his chest with both hands.

"I'm not...I don't..." Angeline stammered and backed away.

Juno stood and began to follow Angeline.

Scorpio withdrew but never dropped his gaze from her face.

He winked at her before he turned and walked away.

41

Another flashback for Angeline

Angeline drove home in a daze.

When she got home she was relieved to see Cricket was gone.

She collapsed into the chair and let out her breath. She ran her fingers through her hair and shook her head.

Pushing the curtain aside, she looked up the driveway. Angeline couldn't sit still. When she jumped up from the chair, she startled the dog.

"Let's go to the store, Juno. I need some dinner."

She went to the bedside table where she had left her notepad earlier and there was a hand drawn mealy bug on the top paper.

'Keeping Secrets'? What was that supposed to mean? Did Cricket think she was keeping secrets from him? Did he think she had some secret life she was hiding from him? She was simply going to a freaking Barter Faire and meeting interesting people.

Her days had suddenly gotten brighter and more fun. She had new friends and she even had a new dog. There was a little pang of guilt when she thought of how she had acquired Juno, but otherwise, there was no secret keeping going on here.

Angeline brushed her hand over her bruised lips. That thing with Scorpio. Her heart pounded with the memory. It was just a moment. She wouldn't let it happen again.

I mean really.

Angeline ripped the top page off the pad and drew her own message back to him. Horsefly. Yes, he was being needy and it really turned her off.

Angeline got back into the car and took off to see the Fairy Congress. She would stop at the deli on the way.

Juno rode in the backseat. She enjoyed looking out the window and loved going for a ride. Angeline rolled the back window down a little after she parked in the shade. Juno stuck her nose out, enjoying the smells coming from the grocery store.

Angeline ran into Hanks Grocery and grabbed what she needed. When she got back to the car from the store, she had a collar and leash, some dog treats and a bowl. Angeline took the old blanket out of the trunk, folded it carefully into a bed and laid it on the seat. Juno was licking her face and smelling the bags, trying to get her nose inside while Angeline unpacked.

"Here's a bowl, here's some food, and I got you treats! Yes I did. Yes I did." The blanket was already in a heap on the floor of the car.

She suddenly felt that swirling sensation. She set the bags on the seat and sat down with her legs out the back door. Juno leaned against her back, sitting happily with her new friend, snuffling her hair and neck. But Angeline was seeing her Granny's back yard.

She saw the garden, the back porch, and the fruit trees. She could even hear the screen door slam as the dog bounded out from the kitchen and down the back stairs.

"Come here, Rags! Come on!" She called.

"Ready for dinner? I got you some leftovers tonight. Yes I did. Yes I did."

Oh, shit how was she going to stop this?

She tried to get up but her mind was so foggy and dazed she could barely manage to put her legs in and close the back door. She didn't want to have a breakdown in public. She laid her head on Juno's back. Juno sat very still. The mood had changed quickly in the car and Juno picked up on it.

I'm in a car. I'm in a parking lot of the grocery store. I'm going to drive to the fairgrounds and see Magpie and we can talk.

She began to breathe consciously in an out very slowly. Juno lay down on the seat; Angeline laid her head next to the dog and continued to breathe.

"Angel, have you done your homework?"

"Yes."

Angeline came back into the house. "Did I get anything in the mail?"

"No, honey."

Why didn't her mother write to her? She hadn't called. Was she even still alive? Could she be in jail? She grieved for her mother and Garcia. She still didn't know if she was kidnapped or if her mom really gave her away.

Slam!

She pictured a heavy steel door in front of the memory and held out her hand and slammed it shut. This time it worked. She spent a few more minutes clearing her head and looking around before she got into the driver's seat and started the car.

42

Tick meets Melody

Tick left the fairgrounds and went back to his hotel. When he found out there were no other vacancies, he moved the coffee pot to the bedside table. Getting out his file, Tick checked off from his list of what he had accomplished that day. He added pages of notes and made a new plan to track this guy down. Tick had spoken to several people at the Faire but no one had seen Raymond. Could he be looking in the wrong place? No time for self-doubt, when he had a hunch, he went with it. He didn't get to this position by good looks alone.

Tick finished his paperwork and headed down to the Pub. Maybe someone had seen the guy by now. Besides, it was time for dinner.

"Hulk's here again." Patrick informed Andrew.

Andrew was in the kitchen trying to fill in for the line cook, who hadn't shown up for the third time.

"Where is that damn cook!" Andrew slung a pot across the drain board and then addressed Patrick, "Who's here?"

"US Marshal. I haven't seen the cook." Patrick answered both questions at once.

"What does he want? I'm buried under an order for twelve...can't help him."

The play was out, that meant they were going to get slammed.

"He wants to eat, but I thought you should know," *Jeez, he was in a bad mood*. Patrick left the kitchen and returned to mixing drinks at the bar.

Hulk was showing Scorpio's photo to the 12-top table and asking them if this guy looked familiar.

"I've never seen him," a blond said. The picture got passed around the table. The redhead thought Hulk was really cute.

"Thanks for your help," he told them and went back to sit at the bar.

The redhead followed him and went to the restroom. When she returned, she stood beside him until she had his attention.

"Are you some kind of agent or something?"

"Yes, ma'am, I am."

The redhead twirled her hair and tried to think of something that would get his attention. She didn't see a ring.

"Do you live here?" Red asked.

"I live in Renton."

"Ooh, cool. I have friends in Seattle, do you know them?"

"I think I might know them, what are their names?"

"Jerry and Katrina."

"What part of town do they live in?"

"Lynwood," she answered.

"That's what I thought. I know them. They live in my neighborhood. I live in Lynwood."

"Awesome!"

Tick didn't know why he was pulling her leg, but he hadn't talked with a beautiful woman in a long time and wanted to take full advantage of it.

The red haired woman sat down on the stool beside him and crossed her long legs. Patrick was watching the whole thing with amusement.

"What's your name?" he asked.

"Melody."

"My name's Tim Blick. People call me Tick."

"Oooh, Tick, that means stubborn. Are you stubborn?"

He raised his eyebrow. What was she talking about?

"Well, I always get my man."

"Haven't you read that bug book?"

"I don't have much time for reading, ma'am."

She liked it when he called her that.

"It's called The Language of Insects, it's all about insects and their symbolic meanings. Tick means stubborn. I'm a firefly, 'luminous and playful.'"

He signaled Patrick for another drink for the two of them.

"So, firefly, what's the good word?"

Her smile lit up and she looked at him, "Well, I always get my man, too."

43

The healing tent

Angeline needed to talk to Magpie. There was a sweet wisdom about her that Angeline knew she could trust. As she drove to the Barter Faire, Angeline decided that she wanted to live in Utopia. She felt like this was where she was supposed to be. Would Cricket agree?

When she got to the grounds this time, Angeline looked for Magpie right away. No one was at the bus. She left Juno there with some food and water and the pup settled right down under the bus where she was accustomed to sleeping.

It was around dinnertime but Angeline wasn't hungry. She wandered through the crowd of people and headed for the carved bridge that spanned the creek. She was intent on her mission and so didn't see that Scorpio had spotted her and was following at a distance. A few folks recognized her and wanted to chat about their new tattoos. She was polite, but cut their conversations short. She was on a mission to find Magpie.

The music was ever-changing as she stepped past colorful swirls of dancers and players. Flutes, guitars, a concertina, a hammer dulcimer, beautiful music accompanied her on her way. It was a mellow evening. Everyone was happy and they were grouping up in different camps. Many were heading for the fairy tent for the main event of the night. First the Fairy ceremony, then the Fairy and Human Parade, then the acoustic concert and then drumming. All day long there had been workshops and circles. There was going to be a Dance for Universal Peace at sunset.

She wandered past the areas spread out with signs designating the different areas. Healing-gifting area, kitchen, tea kitchen, lounge, dining area, information booth, children's area, first aid, costuming, and vendor booths.

The first aid tent was busy that afternoon with the usual bee stings and sunburns. A young woman dressed in a dark blue batik wrap-around skirt was applying peppermint essential oil on the temples of an older woman who had been complaining of a headache. The nurse had given the woman some valerian root extract and was using peppermint rub on her temples.

When the nurse had finished, she walked to the makeshift supply cabinet and searched for the ginger to administer to a young boy who was suffering from a stomachache.

Angeline walked past the vendor booths where they were selling everything from flower oils and singing bowls to fairy wings.

She saw Magpie talking to Kristin at the craft table.

Magpie looked up and saw her. "Hey Angel! Come on over here," Magpie motioned her to join them. She gratefully sat down next to her. The girls were making birdhouses.

"Wanna make a fairy house?" Kristin was gluing rhinestones onto a tiny house that had feathers and other embellishments. Magpie was holding the baby.

"Why not?" She figured it would be a good distraction and she had never made a fairy house before.

"Don't look now, but someone's watching you."

"Really?" Angeline wanted to look. She felt a rush of adrenaline.

Magpie nodded her head.

"Is he coming over here?"

"No."

She started on her fairy house and painted insects all over it. It actually was a fun project.

"How old is your baby?" Angeline asked.

"Five months. Her name is Glow."

They looked at Glow who was sleeping in her sling.

"Cool house," Kristin commented.

They continued working and Angeline felt her stress lifting. She still had to talk to Magpie but she didn't feel so panicked about it.

"I've been having flashbacks," she told the girls in a low voice.

Magpie nodded, encouraging her to go on. She had Kristin's full attention. When Angeline didn't say anything else, Kristin asked her, "What do you want to do about them?"

"I want them to go away," she set down her paintbrush and looked at them.

"You can work through them if you want," Kristin told her.

"I don't want to think about my past. It's over. What good would it do?"

"I know it's a scary thought, but it works. You can go through the memory and process it with someone to guide you through it. Then it won't hurt you anymore."

Angeline got up and walked away from the table. She stood in the grass, and looked down, wrapping her arms around herself.

Magpie and Kristin got up and stood behind her. She felt an arm around her shoulder and let herself be led to the Healing Tent. There were streamers of all colors hanging from the outer walls and strings of flowers wound around the tent poles.

Angeline looked in. It didn't look too intimidating. There were stations set up for massage, and little plushy chairs set up in chat circles. A woman in a fluffy candy pink dress was walking around offering tea and snacks.

Magpie and Kristin followed Angeline through the door. Angeline sat in a plushy chair and when they were all seated she said, "So how do I do this?"

"Let's push our chairs closer," Magpie said.

"Let's get some tea," said Kristin.

"Smell this," said Magpie. She pulled a little vial from her Virgin of Guadalupe shoulder bag. It was healing oil she carried around at all times. You never knew when you might need it.

"Tell us about your memory," said Kristin.

"I'm in the back yard with Granny in the garden. A man comes to the gate and they are arguing. Then she lets him in. Then we are in the kitchen talking at the table and the man tells us that my mom doesn't want me." Angeline sounded so matter of fact, but then her face crumpled and she put her head on her arms and sobbed.

Magpie and Kristin came to her and knelt on the floor next to Angeline's chair. They hugged her. They had tears in their eyes as they waited for her to finish.

"I'm so sorry," Magpie said in her ear. She held up her healing vial again.

44

Deja the healer

"Do you want to tell us about how you came to live with your Granny?" asked Magpie.

"I was in the river. I had just left the treehouse and Mom and Garcia were still sleeping."

Kristin and Magpie looked at each other.

"You lived in a treehouse?"

Angeline nodded. Normally, she didn't talk to people about this, because this was the reaction she usually got.

"How did that work?"

"Well, we were in the forest near Chicken Creek. In the Independence Mountains in Northern Nevada. The treehouse was big enough for all three of us."

"Have you ever gone back?" Magpie asked.

"No. I've never thought about it."

"Did you ever see your mom again?" Kristin was curious.

"No."

"What else happened that day?" Magpie said.

"Granny came up and sat on the bank and talked a little bit. She had sandwiches. She said she had seen my mom and it was alright for me to stay the weekend at her house."

Angeline took a deep breath and composed herself. Magpie took her hand.

The baby woke and sat in her mama's lap watching the women and reaching for her toes.

"It was my fault. I should never have gotten in the car with her. I should have run back to the tree house and made sure it was okay."

Magpie looked around the tent. She saw what she was looking for. "I'll be right back." She said.

Kristin and Glow sat by Angeline waiting for Magpie to come back.

Magpie returned hand in hand with a young girl.

"Honey, you remember Deja. She came with us on the Starry Night bus."

Angeline looked up to see a young girl with gossamer dragonfly wings: Messenger of the gods.

"Of course I do."

"Deja, would you sit here with Angeline for a little while and talk to her?" Magpie asked.

Kristin wrapped Glow in the sling and Magpie stood up.

Deja sat down next to Angeline in the cozy chair circle.

On her way out, Magpie said, "We'll be close by. Don't worry. We'll be back soon."

Angeline was confused. She looked at Deja and wondered what she was supposed to do.

"Did you ever figure out how to juggle?" Angeline asked, trying to compose herself and make conversation.

Deja laughed and stood up. She untied the scarves she had around her waist and began tossing them into the air.

"Good job!"

"I also learned how to walk on stilts; I've been practicing all day."

"That's great, I can't wait to see."

"Why are you in here?" asked Deja as she sat down again. "Did something bad happen?" She was kicking her bare heels against the chair.

"Why do you ask that?" asked Angeline.

"This is the healing tent. Is that why you're here?"

Angeline was going to wave it off. She would usually push it away and move on. But something about the tone of voice she heard from Deja made her take it seriously this time.

"Yes," she admitted, "something bad happened."

Deja leaned in and whispered, "You can tell me. I know about bad things. I can help you."

Angeline looked at the girl curiously. She was sitting very seriously with dragonfly wings, looking ready for Halloween, and saying she could help.

"How can you help me?"

Deja closed her eyes and brought her hands to her chin in a fist, elbows on knees. She sat that way for so long that Angeline thought she might have hurt her feelings. But since she couldn't think of anything to say, she waited to see what happened next.

"You're going to live here," the young girl said.

"Really?"

Deja opened her eyes and asked, "Do you have a dog?"

"I got one today."

"Your dog is very brave."

"What else?"

"You should change your name."

Angeline laughed. What was this all about?

"To Calliope."

"Like the organ at the circus?"

"No, like the daughter of Zeus."

"I should change my name to Calliope and I am moving to Utopia and my dog is very brave. Anything else?"

"It's not your fault."

Angeline collapsed with her face in her hands and sobbed quietly. Deja knelt beside her and rubbed Angeline's knee with her little hand. She began crying too, tears running down her face, Deja knew grief. Heartache knew no boundaries of age. Deja had learned how to heal others because of her own sorrow. Deja would stay for as long as Calliope needed her.

45

Scorpio stalking Angeline

Scorpio waited outside the tent, not wanting to be noticed. What were they doing in there?

Scorpio looked around at the vendors in the field, they were even weirder than the last bunch. They were selling fairy wings, healing oils, flags, and singing bowls.

"What the hell is this?" Scorpio picked up the brass bowl.

"These are good for meditation and personal well-being," said a man who smelled like sweat and garlic. "See, listen to this," he took the bowl from Scorpio and tapped it with a striker reverently and it rang like a bell. Scorpio didn't feel anything.

"This one is made in the mountains of Nepal." He held it up and showed the little pillow underneath. "You can choose the design of your pillow."

Scorpio shook his head and walked away. This was a bizarre place to be. Only a week ago he was in a cell dodging guards and wishing he had a cigarette, daring to dream that one day he would be out. Now he was in a yard full of fairies listening to a man strike a gong. He paced while he waited for Angeline to come out of the tent.

"Do you want to come with me to the circle of peace?" He looked up and saw a man in his 20's wearing a serape.

"No I do not, why don't you people leave me alone?"

He should leave. He would get some dinner and go back to the bus.

Then Scorpio saw her coming out of the tent with a young girl dressed like a dragonfly. All he noticed after that was the way her lavender dress clung to her, flowing to her calves. He was admiring her cleavage and her bare feet with pink toenails. Oh baby. He began to walk over when he saw her merry maidens approach from the other side.

46

Dance of Peace/Fight of Chaos

"How are you?" said Magpie, slipping an arm around Angeline.

She was quiet as she walked with the girls. Deja never left her side.

"Let's get our fairy houses," said Kristin and they started for the craft tent.

Magpie looked up and saw the white flags set up in the Fairy meadow and she realized what they needed to do next.

She walked right past the craft tent and the girls followed her to the circle of peace flags.

Scorpio watched the women walk to the far meadow and stop in the middle of a circle of white flags. What the hell were they going to do now? He wanted to talk to Angeline. Well he wanted to do more than talk.

There were others gathering around; musicians, dancers, people with streamers on sticks swirling in the air. The Dance of Universal Peace was about to begin. Angeline was silent as she took a streamer from the tall clay pot and joined the dancers. It was meditative, it was sacred, and it was joyous. Angeline held her streamer aloft, she felt so light and free. Angeline's memories were small; they held no power over her anymore. The music was sweet; she heard flutes and drumming. There was a beautiful woman dressed like Athena who walked among the dancers anointing them with oil. Angeline accepted a touch on her forehead and smelled the sandalwood. The whole world was fragrant. She lifted her face to the sky, eyes closed, and danced.

Scorpio was really interested now. He watched this woman who looked like a goddess twirl and dance a sensuous dance. She was so sexy he couldn't keep his eyes off her. He wanted to grab her.

"When people eat, dance and pray together, the world finds peace," said a man who was suddenly standing behind him. He jumped out of his skin. No one sneaks up behind Scorpio.

"Get away from me, buddy," he growled.

"We are all brothers here, man. Come and join the Dance of Universal Peace."

"I said get away from me" Scorpio pushed him away and the man tripped and lost his balance. A few people backed away, surprised at the sudden violence.

"That ain't right, man," said a voice. Another held out his hand and helped the guy up. He looked at Scorpio, "Mellow out, brother."

"Don't tell me what to do!" he yelled and pushed that guy, too. This guy didn't fall over. He cocked his arm and punched Scorpio in the solar plexus. Scorpio bent over, and clutching his middle, he fell onto his side gasping for air.

The crowd pushed back to allow some room, forming a circle.

Oh shit, how had he left himself open for that? He didn't expect to have to defend himself at a fucking fairy dance. Scorpio's anger rose up as he caught his breath. A roaring came from his throat and he jumped up swinging.

The man who decked Scorpio was still standing there. The man knew this jerk needed to be subdued before there was any more trouble. He would have to play the bouncer at this party. Pulling his chin up in a gesture to the guys at the back of the circle, they stood behind Scorpio at attention, waiting to grab him. Scorpio had been outnumbered before. He didn't care. They were speaking his language now.

The circle got tighter as the confrontation continued. Scorpio stood with fists clenched, facing the challenger.

"You better get the hell out of my way," Scorpio said through clenched teeth. "I'll get on you and I ain't gonna stop."

"What's your name?" Challenger asked suddenly.

"You don't need to know my name, fucker. I'm gonna take you down!" Scorpio screamed in his face.

"Socrates says the battles we fight are on the inside," he spoke calmly and nodded his head at the waiting men. They grabbed Scorpio from behind. There were too many of them for him to fight back. They had his arms behind his back. Scorpio's legs were kicking and they grabbed those too. They would take him to the river and cool him off, far away from the Dance of Universal Peace.

47

Tick & Melody leave the bar

Tick was having a fun time with Melody. She was getting drunk and he was watching. He could tell she would go back to the hotel with him, but meanwhile it was fun sitting here with a pretty woman shooting the breeze.

"Do you have a gun?"

"What kind of question is that?" Tick asked her.

"Well, if you're an agent you would have a gun," he noticed her eyes starting to go in different directions. "Oooh, I wanna see your badge."

He flipped his wallet open and showed her, Melody gasped.

"I bet you have some handcuffs somewhere…"

"What are you doing now?" Tick asked her as she grabbed a napkin and pulled a pen from her purse.

"I've got something for you," Melody showed him the drawing.

"What is that?" he was confused.

"A fruit fly."

"Looks like a red dot."

"Silly, that's what a fruit fly looks like."

He held it and looked at her.

"Why is this for me? What does it mean?"

"Don't you know about the language of insects? It means 'life is fleeting.' In other words, live like there's no tomorrow. That's my insect."

"I thought you said you were a firefly."

"Oh, yeah. Well, we should live like there's no tomorrow anyway."

"I guess mine is a Tick," he said.

She laughed and bit on her cocktail straw. "That means stubborn."

He set his hand on her knee and looked straight into her eyes.

"I can be stubborn."

She tipped her glass to finish the drink and ice fell on her face.

"Are you ready to go?" she said.

"Do you need to tell your friends?"

"Honey, you're the one with the handcuffs."

She waved at her friends on the way out.

48

Scorpio & the Monk

"Shall we call the cops?" asked the guy who was standing in the river, wrestling with the hothead.

Scorpio immediately calmed down and regained his senses. He realized he probably just blew his cover. How could he have been so stupid?

Bouncer guy loosened his choke-hold a little to see if this wild man was trying to trick him. Neither one moved. The circle of men who were watching stayed still. Everyone was wet. All you could hear was the splashing of water in the creek.

"Are you okay, buddy?" He still didn't know this man's name.

"Don't call me buddy."

"What will you do if I let you go?" the man asked.

"I'm going back to camp and change out of these wet clothes. I'm done." He was humiliated and humbled. He should be mad, but the mention of police took all the fight out of him. He was exhausted. He could sleep for two days.

"The battles that you fight are on the inside," Bouncer said again as he held out his hand and helped Scorpio up. Scorpio let him.

"I'm going back to the camp now."

The witnesses began to disburse. The show was over.

"Are you going to be okay, Man?" said a guy dressed like a monk. He reached out his hand to pat Scorpio on the arm.

"Yes, I'll be fine," he shrugged his arm away.

Monk followed him as he walked away from the crowd. God, all these people would remember what he looked like. Scorpio had to leave immediately.

The two were silent as they walked together.

"Really, you don't have to follow me."

"I want to know that you're okay," he said with no ulterior motive.

Scorpio had never been followed by a monk before, it felt a little strange, but he was too tired to care.

He thought that everyone would be looking at him because he was drenched, but he didn't stand out any more than anyone else. Especially compared to that peacock man on stilts.

"You don't have to fight the inner battle anymore," the Monk interjected.

"Oh Jeez. What now?"

"You think I've always been this way," said Monk, "but I haven't. I found peace in my life.

"Are you going to give me some religious crap?"

"Well, I am dressed like a monk."

"What kind of religion are you going to try to convert me to?" Scorpio wished he had a cigarette.

"The religion of the Higher Power."

Scorpio couldn't shake this guy. He was wet down to his skin and humiliated. He wouldn't take this crap in prison but the outside world was really different. Could he really make it on the outside?

"I'm not interested in your interpretation of the world."

"So what's your name, anyway?"

"Scorpio."

"That's what I thought."

That stopped him in his tracks. Every molecule in his body was on alert. This guy knew his name?

Finally, monk got his attention.

"There's a guy passing your picture around."

Scorpio looked around quickly. "Was he wearing motorcycle gear? Was he bald?"

Monk nodded.

"Oh shit! Are you gonna turn me in?"

"Why would I turn you in?"

Scorpio squinted at the guy and really looked at his face.

"Are you a real monk?"

"Not in the 'go to seminary' sense of the word."

"So what's your name?" Scorpio and monk began to walk again.

"Octavius."

"Yeah, right." Scorpio said.

"I know your name. Scorpio the scorpion: aggression and deceitfulness. The sign of Judas in astrology."

"So which one are you?" Scorpio tested him.

"The bee."

"Have you got a cigarette?"

He slipped his hand into the inner folds of his robe and produced a cigarette and a match and handed them to Scorpio.

"You don't have to live up to your name," said Octavius, "you can choose to change at any time. The scorpion is also tough and resilient. You can develop the positive character of your moniker. Scorpions are also the symbol of protection, wisdom, mystery and logic according to Egyptian teachings."

God, this cigarette tasted good, but it made him light headed. This contributed to the sense of well being he suddenly had toward Octavius the Monk. That, and the fact that the Monk was giving him a new outlook on himself. No one had really tried to understand him before. Scorpio really was wise and mysterious, damn straight.

"Is that guy still around? The bald dude?" Scorpio asked.

"He left earlier. Are you in trouble?" Octavius looked at Scorpio as they walked side by side.

"Did you hear about the earthquake in Walla Walla?"

"No. I am set apart from worldly things. Especially current events. I'm just a pilgrim on this road." Octavius folded his hands and tucked them in his sleeves.

"Anyway, I escaped from prison that day."

"Oh dude. That is awesome, what a blessing."

"Damn Straight," he said, throwing his cigarette on the path and stepping on it.

"Okay, so what is your religion again?" Scorpio steered them toward the trees where he would have a better chance of hiding.

"The religion of Higher Power. There is a Creator in this universe. Every culture in the world has a name for the Creator. Simply choose a name from the list."

"That's it?"

"When you look at yourself as a creation of a Higher Power, you look at yourself and everyone differently. Have you ever meditated or prayed? I want to challenge you to talk to the creator."

Scorpio had prayed while he was in prison. Who hadn't? There were a lot of lonely hours, with layers upon layers of hours to fill when he wasn't sleeping.

Scorpio started out talking to himself, but soon began talking to God like he had when he was a child. Scorpio thought of the years he had been unfairly punished sitting in that tiny cell, banished from the real world.

Year after year, days without end, listening to the constant clamor of the other inmates, that noise that never stopped, hanging with the losers of society, his new peers.

Scorpio sat down on a stump in the woods. There were circles of people here and there. He could smell pot smoke and hear low laughter and camaraderie all around him. He picked up a stick and broke it into small pieces while he thought.

Monk stayed silent and let him reflect. He could tell that something was changing in this wounded soul. He talked to his God while Scorpio processed his thoughts.

"I choose Scarab."

"Virility, courage, strength and resurrection of soul," said Monk.

Octavius reached again into his robe and held out his hand to Scorpio.

Scorpio hoped it was another cigarette.

"What is it?" There wasn't a lot of light in the woods now. The summer sun was almost gone.

Scorpio held out his hand and Monk dropped a stone into it.

"A rock?" Scorpio looked at it closely. There was a fossil in the middle of the flat piece of sandstone. It was a scarab.

He looked at monk. "How did you do that?"

"Scorpio, your life just changed."

Octavius got up and disappeared into the shadows of the cedar grove.

49

Cricket & Brad at the Pub again

"Let's go for a drink," Brad said to Cricket, "I'm not ready to go home yet."

"Sounds good to me," Cricket was game.

They got to the pub and as they were going in, they saw the big guy from the hike.

"What's up? Brad said.

"Hey," Tick nodded and went out the door with a redhead.

"What's up, Patrick?" Brad said as they sat at the bar.

"Did you see the Hulk? He's passing around a picture of some guy," Patrick answered.

"Yep, we saw him on the trail up to Blue Lake today. He showed us a picture, too."

"Who is this guy?"

"We think he's a criminal of some sort."

"I figured that," said Patrick as he poured two beers from the tap. "I wonder why this guy would be here in Utopia."

"He didn't give us any details."

"So, I can't wait to hear the lecture about your book," he said to Cricket.

"I'll be at the bookstore in two weeks, then here at the beginning of September."

"I like it so far," Patrick said. "I think I'm a wooly bear. You know, congenial."

"I could see that," said Brad.

Cricket picked up his beer. He liked to talk about his book but he was distracted by the fact that he hadn't seen much of Angeline for two days. When he did see her, they weren't getting along. He should go home and see if she was there yet.

"You ever been to the Barter Faire?" Cricket asked Patrick.

"I used to trade T-shirts," he answered as he washed beer glasses.

Cricket looked at Patrick, "My wife is doing tattoos there."

The bartender wiped his hands, "People will love the tattoo thing there," he replied.

"Look," Patrick continued, "There's going to be some dancing and special speakers. Everyone talks about world peace. There's a healing tent, which I've worked in before."

"I hope this helps her," Cricket said reluctantly.

Patrick hung up his bar rag and gave Cricket his attention.

Cricket told him about Angeline's abduction as a child, and how they couldn't seem to get along lately.

"She never told me about her childhood, I don't know why she would keep something so important from me."

"Sometimes people don't really want to remember their past," said Patrick. "They think it's easier to ignore it and move on. What people don't realize is that it hurts them more in the long run if they don't process the pain and resolve it once and for all. Bringing memories into the light of day will make them less powerful."

"I can see her suffering but I don't know how to help," Cricket replied.

"Encourage her to talk about her memories, listen and support her. If she wants to see someone, I have a good referral. But let her take the lead, give her a little leeway and be patient. She'll probably be moody until this passes."

Cricket was going to be patient with her. He would spend time doing his own thing until she came home. This Faire would be over tonight anyway, so they could spend some time together starting tomorrow.

“I gotta go,” he said when he finished his beer, “I’ve been gone all day and I need to get some things done.”

“Later, dude.” Brad raised his glass.

50

Cricket's new resolve

Cricket stopped for gas at the small store on the way back to the cabin. He went in to pay and saw a display of scarves, which included a sweet bandanna, covered with hand painted songbirds. He bought the bandanna, along with some candy bars and a magazine for Angeline. It was time to stop all this nonsense and work out whatever it was they were squabbling about.

It was after nine when Cricket pulled into the driveway, and he saw that Angeline wasn't there yet.

He slammed the car door and went inside to see if she had been home that day.

Turning on the kitchen light, he set the bag of gifts down when he saw the pad of paper on the table.

Horsefly?

She was accusing him of being needy?

He grabbed the pencil and scribbled out the drawing and threw the pad across the kitchen.

They had a deal. Angeline was supposed to spend time with him on this vacation.

He should drive out there right now and make her come home.

The memory of the conversation he had with Patrick came to him.

"Let her take the lead, give her some leeway and be patient" Patrick had advised.

He took a deep breath and let it out. The Faire will be over tonight, he reminded himself. She was getting the healing she needed. I'll just have to spend time with her after tomorrow.

Cricket woke to an empty bed, Angeline still hadn't returned. He hastily threw on his clothes from the night before as he tried her on the cell phone. The phone hadn't worked before; he didn't know why he was wasting his time. He didn't want to wait to see his wife.

He was going to drive out to the fairgrounds and see for himself what was going on.

51

Tick & Melody

It was morning and Melody was sleeping off the appletini's she had at the pub. Tick didn't mind. He liked looking at Melody as he went through his notes. The coffee pot gurgled and spit out its meager pot of coffee on the bedside table. He reached over and retrieved the powder packets from the container and ripped them open into a paper cup.

"Creamer. Really?" Tick said to himself as he tried to read the tiny print of ingredients on the packet.

Melody yawned and stretched and Tick was aroused again seeing her naked body rising under the sheet.

"Did we have fun?" she asked.

"I sure did," he answered.

"Now I remember," she sat up, "You sure did."

Her hair was a mess, but still beautiful. Melody turned on her side to watch him pour powder into the paper cup and stir the whole mess with a plastic straw.

"I think we can get some better coffee in the lobby," Melody remarked.

"I don't feel like going into the lobby quite yet." He was ready to climb back under the sheets and mess up Melody's hair even more.

"I'll get some," she got up and put on his robe. He watched with fascination as she turned and looked at him mischievously, then slammed the door behind her.

She came back with two ceramic cups of coffee, set them on the dresser and slid out of his robe. She picked up the coffee and handed him one of the cups. He held it in his hand, not taking his eyes off her. He set down the coffee and his notes and stood up in front of her. Melody took a sip while he spanned her waist with his hands. She finally set the cup down on the bed stand and tilted her head back, feeling his kisses on her neck and down her throat. Tick ran his hands over her hips as he bent down and caressed her breasts with his tongue.

When her legs couldn't hold her another minute, she backed toward the bed and lay down while he finished his mission. US Marshal to the bone.

52

"I know that guy"

Tick and Melody were both hungry and he didn't want her to leave yet.

"Breakfast?" he said when he caught his breath.

"Yum. I'd love a big breakfast."

She showered quickly, and then dressed in her green silk blouse and black skirt and put on her black strappy sandals. Melody swept her hair into a clip and was ready to leave the hotel.

Tick was looking at the notes in his lap while he waited for her to get ready.

"What kind of project are you working on?" asked Melody.

"Remember the photo I showed you last night?"

"Not really. It was dark and I was a little distracted," she said.

"I'm looking for a guy that busted out of prison," Tick showed her the picture again.

"I know him," she took the picture from his hand and handed it back.

He was surprised to say the least.

"You know him? How do you know him?"

He noticed her slight hesitation before she answered.

"I saw him at the Barter Faire. He was hanging around that bus with all the blue swirls painted on it."

"I knew it!" He banged his fist on the arm of the chair and stood up suddenly, startling her.

"I've got to get back there."

"But what about breakfast?"

He peeled off a twenty and handed it to her.

"Why don't you just leave it on the dresser?"

He ignored the insinuation.

"I'm getting in the shower real quick and then I've got to go back," he wondered why she stood there with her hands on her hips.

"Did you want to come, too? You could identify him."

Melody couldn't decide, she had already packed up her booth and brought it all back to her friend's house to store in the shed.

Tick was already in the shower. Melody hollered at him through the door, "Okay, I'll go! Can you drop me off at my car on the way?"

"I'll be right out!" he yelled back.

She finished her coffee while she waited and pocketed the twenty on principle.

"Do you live here?" he was asking as he drove her to her car.

"I live in Montana. I have a studio where I make renaissance clothing."

"Who buys renaissance clothing?" he asked.

"Lots of people. I take trunk loads of clothing to renaissance fairs and barter fairs and any gathering where people want to get in touch with their sense of play. All children enjoy dressing up. Most of us leave it behind when we become adults."

"Do you make pirate clothes?"

"My pirate clothing is the most popular. I go to pirate festivals all the time."

"There's my car," she pointed down the street at the blue '89 Mustang.

"Are you following me?"

"I'll be right behind you."

He waited for her to get in and start the car then they took off for the fairgrounds.

53

Angeline reveals her future

The sun was rising and the three women were stretching and waking in various degrees as the warmth hit the tent. Baby Glow was cooing as Kristin lay on her side and nursed her. Mother and babe gazed at each other. Angeline and Magpie were soon murmuring their good mornings and rolling over. Angeline was clear headed and happy.

"Good Morning, little Glow," Magpie said to the baby.

"She says Good Morning back," said Kristin.

They were all sitting up now, Angeline digging in a cooler for something to eat.

"God, I love this," she said to her friends.

"Sorry you didn't get home last night, but I'm glad you could stay with us."

"Cricket will understand. I tried his cell, but I forgot there's no service here." She didn't feel guilty; she was so content that no negative feelings could touch her this morning.

"Angeline, I'm really going to miss you," said Kristin.

"Calliope. I changed my name last night."

"Tell me about your meeting with Deja," said Magpie. "She is such a little healer."

"She said I would live in Utopia, which I was already contemplating. Then she said I should change my name to Calliope, like the daughter of Zeus."

"Cool! She is the lover of the war god, Ares."

"Then she said my dog was very brave."

"Juno, the warrior goddess. I don't doubt that she is," said Magpie. "Wow, you have a real adventure going on here, my friend."

"All I know is that I am right where I'm supposed to be at this moment. That is a foreign concept for me."

The women crawled out of the tent and started a fire to make some coffee.

54

Scorpio's new religion

Scorpio sat up when he smelled the smoke from the campfire and looked out the bus window. There they were, Charlie's Angels, sitting by the fire thick as thieves. He got up and dressed in the same jeans and t-shirt he got from the guy at the barn owl stall two days ago. Was that only 2 days ago?

"What's your t-shirt say?" asked Magpie when Scorpio neared the fire.

"John Wayne, American Legend," he stretched it out so they could see.

"Where were you last night? Did you go to The Congress?"

"Shit no, that's not my thing."

"Calliope, could you get some potatoes and onions and garlic from the bus? Bring the whole box, there's not much left."

"Calliope?" Scorpio snorted.

Calliope got up and headed for the bus, Juno stood up, anticipating her breakfast.

"Is that your name now?" Scorpio called as she walked away.

She turned to him; "I changed it last night."

"I changed my religion," he tried on the words to see how they felt.

The women looked at him, waiting for an explanation.

Calliope poured dog food into the new dish with a clatter. Juno's tail whipped back and forth as she stuck her nose into the food and gobbled her breakfast.

When Calliope stood up, she turned toward him, waiting to hear more from Scorpio.

"You know that monk that hangs out?" he asked.

"I haven't seen him," said Kristin.

"Me neither," said Magpie.

"Well, anyway, he gave me this last night," he unfolded his fist and presented the fossil to his audience with pride.

"Scarab: resurrection of the soul," Magpie interpreted.

"Let me see," Calliope asked. She came near and he handed her the stone.

"That is awesome." The girls were huddled around Scorpio, wanting to know more.

-"Did the monk give that to you?"

-"What was his name?"

-"What religion are you now?"

They were all talking at once.

"His name was Octavius. He talked to me about my Higher Power and seemed to know me without having ever met me before."

Magpie nodded knowingly. Glow bounced up and down on her mama's lap and reached for the stone.

"What are you going to do now?" Magpie asked.

"Can you take me down the road when you leave?"

"Sure," she was still curious about his conversion.

"Calliope, you forgot to get the box," Magpie pointed out.

"I'll get it," Scorpio went to the bus, but still watched for Harley guy. He thought if he laid low he could make it until they left that day.

55

Tick & Melody on their way to the Faire

Tick led the way and Melody followed behind as they drove down the road to the fairgrounds. She knew where Scorpio was staying, that's for sure. She really didn't want Tick to find out how she knew. That guy had been a jerk to her, like he didn't care at all about her. But oh, he was so good. She turned on the CD player and listened to Janis Joplin the rest of the drive.

Tick was focused on how this was going to play out. Would he confront Raymond directly or surprise him? The Marshal wasn't worried about backup, he could call if he found the guy, this would be an impressive coup when he took the con without help. Tick was highly trained. He smiled at the thought of Melody watching him overpower that scumbag. He shoved Steppenwolf into the CD player and psyched up for the confrontation.

56

Scorpio trapped

Deja crawled out of her tent, "I smell bacon!" She yawned aloud and stretched.

"Hey, Calliope. Hey Magpie and Kristin. Ooooh little Glow! Heya Heya sweetpea." She danced around the group and swirled her finger in Glow's face.

She grabbed a cup and went for the coffee as the women watched her.

"Do you always drink coffee?" Kristin asked.

"No. I thought I'd try some this morning." She poured half a cup and drank it with gusto.

SPEWWWW the coffee sprayed onto the grass as she coughed and sputtered.

"GROSS, how can you drink that stuff?!"

They laughed at her and Magpie began to make her some mint tea.

Deja sat in the grass next to Calliope.

"How are you this morning?" she asked.

Calliope set her hand on the girl's head and stroked her hair.

"I'm doing really well, better than I ever have. Thank you, Deja."

The girl beamed. "I can help heal people. There's something that I can tell about people. I thought everyone was like that until I got older and found out they weren't."

She leaned in and whispered to Calliope, "I know there's something about that hitchhiker that is very sad. He is wounded more than most. I can't talk to him, though, there's something dangerous about him."

"That's Scorpio," she whispered to Deja, "I think you should stay away from him, you're right."

"Juno Juno Juno!" Deja ran towards the dog, then ran away, then towards. She made everyone tired just watching. Juno loved it. She had her paws out far and her head down low.

Juno looked like she was smiling. Then she let out a howl of joy, raising her head high in the air.

Deja and the dog took off running around and around the bus.

While Scorpio was on the bus, he stuck his hand in his pocket and felt the scarab the monk had given him. God might be on his side, God might help him and save him from the cop.

"God, God, let me get away," he chanted to himself as he found the box of food for Magpie. God knows he was innocent and didn't belong in prison. There could be something to this.

When he heard a familiar voice in the camp he quickly peeked out the window to see who it was.

Holy shit it was Montana, and she had that cop with her. He crouched down and hoped his new friends wouldn't rat him out. He couldn't chance another peek, but he really wanted to know what the hell was going on out there. Scorpio's legs were cramping from the position he was in but he didn't dare move, he couldn't give himself away. Scorpio was in such a panic, he could barely see or hear. He shook his head to dodge the panic that attacked him from everywhere at once. He opened his mouth to breathe deeply. He tried to keep his hands from shaking as he set down the apples and yogurt on the floor of the cluttered bus.

The mat was clotted and sticky from a weekend of camping. The bus smelled like hot metal, mold and mice droppings, especially near the floor. The sun was coming through the row of windows, bringing wave after wave of nauseating heat.

57

The women are hiding Scorpio. Again.

When Melody led Tick to the Starry Night camp they saw breakfast cooking on the fire. Scanning the area, he immediately saw four tents but no sign of Raymond. Tick decided on the direct approach. He was a master in martial arts and had years of US Marshal training. Tick didn't scare easily. Raymond had only been an accessory to the liquor store crime. He was going to try the intimidation route and go in directly and grab him. He had his gun, cuffs and badge. What more did he need? He could take this guy, easy.

He checked to see if Melody was watching as he did a quick check for the pistol in his shoulder holster. Exaggerating his movements, he leaned his chin into his radio and shrugged his left shoulder to meet his mouth to the speaker. Tick asked for backup in elaborate code to headquarters.

Headquarters was sending a man from Pendleton, only a half hour away. He didn't need to wait. This would be a walk in the park.

Magpie, Kristin and Calliope recognized him from the day before.

"Wonder if you've seen that guy yet?" asked Tick abruptly. They had lied to him before; he expected a repeat performance.

"We've seen him," Magpie spoke for the group.

"What do you want him for?" She didn't see a clear aura around this man. Or his girlfriend.

She tolerated this Marshal guy yesterday, but give Scorpio a break, he had changed, Scorpio was innocent. The US Marshal wouldn't understand that. "I want to know where you've seen him," Tick answered.

Melody stood there looking around. She held her chin up and set her jaw, her eyes narrowed as she thought about how he used her. Melody was happy to lead the marshal to the camp, see if that fucker called her Montana again.

"Do you want some tea or coffee?" Magpie asked.

58

A shot rings out

Scorpio was hiding on the bus alone, rummaging desperately through the boxes and packs for a weapon. Any weapon would do, he wouldn't go down without a fight. He couldn't go back to prison, *why didn't he leave the camp yesterday*? Scorpio was cornered like a cockroach in this stinking rattletrap. He looked under the seats for a place to hide. His vision was blurred with panic. His brain was shutting down. Scorpio wouldn't give in this time. He would kill that guy trying to take him down.

Time slowed as Scorpio rummaged through clothes and food and instrument cases looking for a weapon. STOP. THINK. *I've got to pull it together here*. His hands were slippery with panic and his mind was racing.

"God, God, let me get away," he prayed.

Then he found a colt .32 hidden in a banjo case, near the headstock.

"Thank you," he whispered.

Scorpio was squatting on the floor of the bus, checking the casing to see if the gun was loaded. Three rounds. Okay, he would stay close to the floor and when that Marshal came to get him, he would be ready.

Deja was running and running around the trees outside the camp, laughing and chasing the dog. Magpie noticed her first and froze as she watched the girl run toward the bus and take a leap onto the steps to get away from Juno.

All heads turned at once, the women didn't know how to stop Deja without blowing Scorpio's cover.

The dog waited at the bottom of the steps whining and barking for Deja to come back.

Tick saw the look on Magpie's face when the little girl ran up the stairs and into the bus. He looked at the bus and then looked at the women again. What was she afraid of? Were they covering for this con? Raymond was on the bus, Tick realized. He looked at Magpie who nodded reluctantly. Now that Deja was on the bus, all bets were off. Conversion or not, he was still an inmate being pursued by a man who would take him back to prison.

Scorpio heard the silence and that was a bad sign. Everyone knew he was hiding on the bus. Concentrating so hard and staring at the front entry of the bus took all his energy. He was on high alert. His hand kept involuntarily clicking the safety of the colt. On. Off. On. He shifted to his heels, then sat and tried to burrow silently into the pile of blankets and backpacks that lay in lazy mounds, carelessly left by the other campers. Click. Click. Click. Changing his restless mind again he stood up. He would face this like a man. He heard the US Marshal run up the stairs in a clatter of pounding feet. Juno barked, warning Scorpio of danger.

Scorpio stood up suddenly and held the gun straight out with both hands, elbows locked and he shot without hesitation.

59

Tick calls to Scorpio

The group of women screamed when they heard the shot, and Juno leapt onto the bus to save Deja. Tick drew his weapon and ran toward the bus.

The windshield was shattered. There was no sound except the barking that echoed out of the cavern of the Starry Night bus.

Magpie and Calliope screamed and grabbed each other in horror. They wanted to rescue Deja, but were not able to get close to the bus.

"Raymond!" Tick hollered up the stair landing.

He could see the driver's seat, the black rubber mat and the broken windshield. The dog was whining but there were no more shots.

"Scorpio!" he commanded again.

Then he heard the little girl's voice. He couldn't make out what she was saying, but he knew she was alive.

"Scorpio, send the girl out!"

Nothing.

60

Deja's story

The man was scared and he shot at her. It startled her and Juno. But Juno was a brave dog, a warrior dog, and barked at the man with the gun. Deja wasn't afraid. She stayed very calm. She looked at her body and didn't see any blood. Nothing hurt except her ears. They rang and rang.

The man in the black t-shirt was shaking. Deja had an idea.

First she patted Juno on the head, "Good girl, Juno, shh." The dog quieted down but never took her eyes off the bad man.

Deja stood still and forced her voice to be calm and sweet. "Hush, Juno." She took the dog's ear between her fingers and rubbed it over and over. It calmed them both.

Deja talked to the scared man in a calm voice. That would always fix things when she lived with her mama.

"I won't hurt you," Deja said quietly.

Scorpio was still shaking as he sat hard on the floor of the bus. He scooted backwards amongst the boxes of clothing and food.

"Me and Juno are going to leave now."

"No. Stay on the bus." Scorpio was holding the gun, but didn't have it pointed at her.

"Why are you scared?" Deja asked.

Scorpio didn't respond.

Deja rubbed Juno's ear.

"Do you have a rock?" she asked.

"What?"

"It has a beetle on it."

"Where do you see that?" Scorpio looked around on the floor.

"In my head."

His mind was clearing as he listened to the little girl. She understood him. She knew he didn't mean to hurt anyone. He was scared. His ears were still ringing but this girl's calm voice cut through his thoughts like the notes of a forgotten lullaby. He took a deep breath.

"What else do you see?"

"You're sitting in a creek," Deja said to him.

"If you want to leave, you can take my hand," she added and held out her hand. Deja had said this to her mama and it worked before, when mama had to go to the hospital.

"I want Angeline," Scorpio said softly.

"I'll go see if I can get her," Deja said in her calmest voice and began bravely to walk to the front of the bus. The windshield was cracked. That must have been where the bullet went.

"No!" Scorpio shouted. Deja froze.

"I want Angeline!" his voice echoed through the bus.

Tick was standing with his body pressed against the outside of the bus, near the doorway, listening hard. Waiting.

"Send out the girl!" he commanded.

Swirls of blue and yellow stood out behind him, the peaceful village of *Starry Night* an ironic background. Where was his backup? Others had gathered nearby but they kept their distance as they watched and whispered questions to each other.

There was a little girl on the bus and a man with a gun.

Had the girl been shot? Who was this guy? Some people were still and quiet, concentrating. Some were praying, lips moving silently, eyes closed. There was whispering and crying, the passing of rumors.

The agent looked behind him at Angeline who took a step forward, focused on him. Scorpio had called her name. She would go in if she had to.

61

Cricket sees his wife

That's when Cricket saw his wife. He saw her stand up straight and tall as she broke from the huddle of women and walk toward the man pressed against the bus with a gun drawn.

Cricket tried to shove through the crowd, but someone grabbed his arm and held him back.

"That's my wife," Cricket said with urgency.

Cricket was confused. What was Angeline doing?

"Wait, my man, there's a hostage situation." A loud whisper in his ear.

The man wouldn't let go and Cricket was afraid to call out.

Tick motioned for Angeline to come close.

Why did the man on the bus call out for his wife? Why was she being sent onto the bus with a man who had a gun?

Cricket tried to break away from the crowd and get to his wife. He would go on the bus in her place; she could be killed.

"Will you send out the girl if Angeline comes in?" Tick shouted to Scorpio. He wanted to get the guy to respond to him. He had many hours of training in hostage negotiation. He was smarter than this asshole.

62

Someone loves you

Deja looked at her captor who sat on the floor of the bus.

"Why do you want to talk to Angeline?" she asked him.

Scorpio didn't answer.

"Let me see your rock," she said suddenly.

Scorpio set down the gun on the green duffel bag that was under the seat and reached into the front pocket of his jeans and pulled out the fossil. He handed it to Deja who was sitting on the edge of the bus seat nearby.

Scorpio reached out to touch Juno.

"She is a really nice dog," he said.

"You gave her to Angeline, didn't you?" Deja studied the rock.

"I love Angeline," he said simply.

"And someone gave this to you," she held the scarab out to him in her outstretched palm.

His heart flipped and adrenaline rushed through his body. A flood so sweet he didn't know what to think. Someone loved him.

"Do you want me to go get her?" Deja asked.

He nodded as he took back the stone and waited for Angeline to come to him.

Tick heard footsteps walking down the aisle of the bus, they were approaching the door and Tick inched closer; hand on his gun. He motioned everyone to back away as he waited to see who would appear in the doorway.

Deja and Juno stood at the top of the stairs all alone. She was holding the dog's ear and was rubbing it in her fingers as they stood there.

"He wants Angeline," she said.

"Come on down here, sweetie," said Tick, "Angeline will be right up."

He spoke loud so Raymond would hear the conversation.

Deja walked down the steps toward Magpie who had her arms out to the little girl.

Magpie picked her up in an embrace and carried her far away, whispering in her ear as they moved toward the trees. Deja began to cry.

Juno followed as they made their way into the woods.

63

Another shot rings out

Angeline walked over to the agent and waited quietly for instruction.

He shook his head no.

She turned to the crowd to see where Magpie had gone and saw Cricket standing at the edge of the crowd, arm held tightly by a civil war costumed man.

As Angeline ran to Cricket, there was a gunshot. Cricket grabbed his wife and stumbled away from the crowd, taking her away from danger. She buried her head in his chest and shook violently.

Tick couldn't assume anything when that last shot rang out. He had to wait or his life could be in danger.

"Raymond!" he yelled from the bottom of the steps.

Finally his backup arrived running across the camp, equipment jangling in the silence, the crowd parting for him. He squatted next to Tick and they spoke quietly but urgently, Tick ran to the other side of the bus to look in the window while his backup stayed by the front door.

A moment later the radio came alive with static and the crowd saw the other cop enter the bus.

Scorpio's body was lying in the middle of the aisle runner. He lay in a heap of bags and boxes on the floor of the bus.

Tick checked his watch as he entered the bus one step behind his backup man. He grabbed his radio and called the Utopia Police to report the time of death before he even approached the body.

64

First Responders arrive

Melody stood and watched from afar, she didn't really know what else to do now. She wanted to stay near Tick. She was kind of attached to him.

The fire engines approached, lights flashing, no sirens. There were three of them, the whole fleet representing Utopia. The men jumped down from the truck wearing yellow slickers, overalls and large boots. The resident EMT approached Tick standing outside the bus and began to ask him questions before he mounted the stairs.

Five cop cars came rushing up, Utopia's whole regiment. The Utopia Police Force got out of their cars and went straight to the crowd outside the bus, asking questions of the eyewitnesses as part of the investigation. There were more uniformed men than any of the fair goers had ever seen in one place.

Many of the participants were starting up their buses and taking their leave. It was Monday and the Barter Faire was over for another year.

There were cops and firefighters all over the bus, measuring, photographing and note taking. Others were canvassing the crowd. Interviewing. Interrogating. Getting the facts. A white van approached, driving through the grassy parking lot, the Umatilla County symbol painted on the side. The coroner had arrived.

65

Calliope's summary

"Are you okay?" Cricket whispered into his wife's ear as he held her.

Calliope nodded her head. She was so stunned by the experience she was still trying to piece it all together.

"What in the world happened?"

"That man escaped from jail last week. He was staying here at the camp and then he started acting crazy."

"Are you ready to go back to the cabin?" he asked her.

"Not yet, the police will need my information before I go. And I want you to meet Magpie, Kristin and Deja and all the friends I've made this weekend," Calliope was going to miss Magpie so much.

They walked out of the trees and toward the river where the others had gathered by the big rock.

Calliope was torn between staying near the bus and getting as far away as she could. She and Cricket moved toward the group of trees where they saw Magpie holding Deja.

"Magpie and Deja have played a big part in my healing this weekend. Deja lives with Magpie as kind of a foster mother."

"Over there is Kristin with baby Glow," she motioned to the young mother and baby who sat near the creek. They were sitting on a rock in the sunshine, Kristin keeping the baby away from the chaos and grief near their camp.

"Kristin lives in Utopia with her husband, Cameron."

Calliope didn't think this was the time to mention that she wanted to move here, yet.

They were walking toward Magpie and Deja as she spoke.

"Are you okay, Deja?" She reached out to hug the teary eyed girl.

"Calliope!"

Calliope? Cricket wondered.

She held the girl for a long time and they both cried again. This would be a very emotional day. The memories of this experience would never go away.

"Cricket, this is my friend Deja."

"Glad to meet you, Deja." He shook her hand.

"Cricket? That's a cool name!"

She thought for a moment, "Good luck and musical," she recited.

"How did you know?" he laughed.

"I am memorizing the bug book."

"What insect have you picked out for yourself?"

"Dragonfly: Messenger of the gods," she replied with seriousness.

Juno burst through the woods and ran to the river and jumped in, bounding and splashing in the shallow water.

"That's my dog," Calliope announced.

Cricket wondered what else was going to happen this morning, what else he didn't know about his wife.

"How did you get a dog?" he asked.

"I traded her for a tattoo," she suddenly got quiet, remembering the incident. How much was she going to reveal to her husband about this weekend?

"Like Jack and the Beanstalk again."

Calliope looked at him expecting his disapproval, but he was smiling.

"Her name is Juno, Warrior Dog."

"She saved Calliope's life, and mine," announced Deja.

Cricket looked at his wife, there was that name again.

"Calliope?"

"I changed my name."

"Alright, how did that happen?"

All the women began to talk at once, but Cricket held up his hand. Obviously this was an exciting moment for all of them, but it was confusing him.

"Why don't you tell me the story?" Cricket was looking at his wife.

"I was in the healing tent, and I was having flashbacks about that time I was taken by Granny…"

"You were having flashbacks?" he responded.

"Then Magpie went and got Deja because she's a healer…"

Cricket looked at Deja.

"And she told me that I was going to live in Utopia, and my dog would be very brave and that I should change my name to Calliope…"

"Like the circus organ?"

"No, like the daughter of Zeus. And that it wasn't my fault."

He kept looking at her for more information. He looked at the other women who were following as though all of this was logical and he was the one who wasn't getting it.

"Look, I can juggle," Deja said suddenly and began to untie the scarves from her waist.

She threw the scarves into the air and walked around flinging and catching the colorful silks.

Kristin had been watching and listening as she and Magpie sat together on the big rock by the creek. Juno shook herself as she climbed out of the creek, and began running around Deja, barking and jumping and trying to catch the scarves as they flew through the air.

Kristin approached the couple, "Your wife has been a wonderful friend to us this weekend. I'm really going to miss her," she reached out for Calliope's hand.

"We're going to be around for a few more weeks. I've got two lectures to do and an Insect Contest to judge."

"Really? Cameron and I go every year. We love the contest!"

"You've got two lectures lined up? That's awesome, Cricket," Calliope said. She turned to Magpie to see what her friend would do next.

"Are you leaving today Magpie? Are they going to let you drive your bus? I wonder what's going to happen?"

"I don't know, Sweetie, I guess we'll find out sometime today. I think I'll have to stay in town for a few days until they sort this out."

They were all looking into the distance at the flashing lights. The ambulance was pulling out, the fire trucks had left, but the police would be in the camp for a long time.

Calliope hugged her friends. "We'll see you guys later," said Calliope as she led Cricket by the hand down the river path. She wanted to talk privately with him and walk by the water.

66

Let's move here. Let's go to Nevada.

"Do I have to call you Calliope?" he asked her. She listened for mocking in his voice, but there was none.

"I would like it if you did, but you don't have to."

"Did you really have a healing?"

"I did. This was the best place for me to be this weekend, I needed this."

Cricket scratched his head. "Well, I guess I'm glad for you, then."

"Thank you."

She turned to him and held both his hands in hers.

"I really do want to move here," Calliope had been afraid to mention it, but might as well get it out.

"I do too," Cricket said.

Calliope let out her breath, not realizing she had been holding it.

He squeezed her hands and drew her into a hug and kissed the top of her head.

"Cricket?"

"Call me Jupiter," she looked up at him and laughed.

"I want to go to Nevada."

"When?"

"Right now, as soon as possible," she said, relieved that he was open to the idea.

"Well, let's get back to the cabin, and make a plan," Cricket said.

"Can you tell me anything more about your idea?" He chose his words carefully as they walked toward the parking lot.

"Just that I have a lot of unanswered questions."

"We've got time before the contest to take a trip," he said.

"Hey, let's go into town and find a place to live," Cricket suggested.

They walked hand in hand out of the woods and back to the camp. Calliope, formerly known as Angeline, was finally ready to talk.

67

Calliope tells her story again

The camp cleared out fast when the cops showed up. No one wanted to hang out much after they arrived. The only people left were the folks from Starry Night camp, only because there was no way to leave. They were witnesses and their bus was now evidence. After each person was interviewed, they took their belongings and hitched into town. The only ones left were Magpie, Deja, Calliope and Cricket. And Juno.

"What are you going to do?" Calliope asked Magpie.

"I've got to find a place for me and Deja to stay for a few days," she replied. "They'll probably release the bus on Wednesday."

"I wonder if Brad would let you stay in one of the cabins at his fiddle camp," Calliope suggested. She didn't think he would turn away a woman and a little girl.

"Come on, we'll give you a ride to the property and see if we can find him."

They all walked to the car. The parking field was almost deserted now. Cricket went to his borrowed car and the girls got into the rental.

Calliope turned on the radio and they drove back to town. The women could hear Deja talking to Juno in the backseat.

"You saved my life, Juno. You beautiful warrior dog," said Deja.

"That's for sure," said Calliope.

"It would be great if we were able to stay at the camp. I'd like to visit a little more," Magpie announced.

"Me, too. But Cricket and I are going to take off for Nevada," Calliope announced.

"When is that?"

"I'm not sure, probably in a day or two."

"Is that where you're from? Where you lived in a tree house?" asked Magpie.

"Yes."

"You lived in a tree house?" came a voice from the backseat.

"I did!" Calliope responded.

"How big was it? Who lived there with you? How old were you?" Deja had a million questions.

Calliope searched her memory for the answers. It had been a long time since she had allowed herself to remember her childhood. Maybe this trip to Nevada would help her to remember.

68

I didn't tell you I was a Rainbow?

Calliope and Cricket were in the cabin preparing chicken for the grill. They hadn't seen Brad yet. Brad was coming over later when he got done feeding and watering the livestock at his ranch. Cricket was apprehensive about Magpie and Deja being on the property. He didn't think Brad would approve; but he kept this to himself.

Calliope was cutting fruit and arranging it on a plate when she began to speak, "The earliest memory I have is my dad playing the guitar and he and my mom singing."

She carried the fruit out to the picnic table and Cricket followed with a plate of hamburger patties to put on the hot grill.

"I remember mom woke me up one night. She told me to be quiet. We were outside in the dark. It was cold. She said we were going on a trip and we went on a bus somewhere."

"What about your dad?" he asked her.

"I don't know where he was. I don't have any other memories of him. She never talked about him again. I don't even know his name."

Magpie and Deja came out with a Frisbee and a bowl of watermelon slices. Juno ran as Deja threw it over and over again.

The three of them sat at the table and watched.

"I remember living in the park in a tent. Then we moved to the tree house. Garcia and mom and I."

"Did you go to school?" Magpie asked, stirring honey into her sun tea. Deja came and sat down. She grabbed a watermelon slice and began eating it.

"I was home-schooled."

"Like me!" said Deja.

"I was supposed to watch out for Granny. They warned me to watch out for her. She was looking for us," Calliope continued.

"That's why I was scared that day when she showed up. She seemed so nice. She had sandwiches. She said my mom had talked to her about me visiting for the weekend."

"I wanted to go back to the tree-house and check in with mom before we left, but Granny just took off."

Tears ran down Calliope's cheeks, but she kept talking.

"My Granny made sure I went to school and she taught me how to grow a garden and how to cook. But I never felt at home there."

"Honey, why didn't you stay in touch with your granny?"

Calliope picked at her fingernail, "I never got over the anger about her taking me away," she said finally.

Cricket checked the meat. Deja was listening very carefully.

"How old were you?" she asked.

"About your age."

"What did you do before? When you lived with your mom?"

"We went to Rainbow gatherings. We were Rainbows."

"What's that?" asked Cricket.

Magpie answered, "They are a group of people interested in world peace that started in the '60s." She looked at Calliope, "I have some friends who still go to the gatherings. Actually, there were some Rainbows at the Faire this weekend."

"I've been out of touch with the group since I was a child," said Calliope, "We used to go to the Regionals and then the National gathering in July every year."

"You know there's a Rainbow Guide?" said Magpie.

"What's that?" asked Calliope.

"You can go on-line and look up people."

She felt a bolt of fear and excitement go through her. Was it possible to find her mother? Did she want to?

Cricket saw the look on his wife's face and the way her body suddenly froze up.

"You don't have to do any of this, Calliope," he used her new name awkwardly; "It's your choice."

She looked at him with a mixture of fear and courage, "I'm going to do this, I really need to."

"I'm behind you all the way," Cricket declared.

"Me, too," said Deja. She laid her hand on Calliope's shoulder.

"I can look up the information for you if you want," Magpie added.

"I'll let you know what I decide to do," she told her new friend.

They served the dinner at the picnic table and Cricket took them all on an insect tour afterward.

"I found a ladybug!" Deja proclaimed. "That means good luck!"

"Hey, can I get a tattoo, Calliope?" she quickly added.

"No, young lady, not until you're older," she answered, "But what would you get if you could?"

"I would get a dragonfly. That's my favorite."

They continued to walk through the field.

69

I've seen you before

"I thought Brad was coming tonight," said Cricket.

They heard his truck come down the driveway, "Speak of the devil," he added.

They waved at him as he came closer to the picnic table. "Did you want some dinner?" said Calliope.

"I got caught up with a calf that needed extra attention tonight," Brad explained.

"Well, dig in, there's plenty left," Calliope offered.

He squinted at Magpie and Deja.

"Are these your visitors?" he jerked his head toward the two as he addressed Cricket.

The group froze like they were playing an awkward game without knowing the rules.

"I've seen you somewhere before," he squinted as he looked at Magpie.

"I don't know where," she responded.

Calliope squirmed and couldn't think of a way to ask if her friends could stay at the camp.

Brad sat at the table. Deja got up and walked over to Magpie and took her hand.

Brad took off his hat and slapped it on the bench, "Well?"

Calliope spoke up, "There was a terrible death at the camp, and Magpie and Deja don't have anywhere to stay until their bus gets released from custody."

"What are you talking about?"

Cricket decided to plead their cause; they weren't like the other hippies from the Faire.

"Brad, this is Magpie and her daughter Deja. We thought they could stay for a few days until they can get a ride back home."

The rancher wiped his face with his kerchief and let loose a suffering sigh.

"How long will that be?"

"We will leave the first chance we get," Magpie finally found her voice.

"Wait," he got up from the table and pulled a ring of keys from his pocket.

He had suddenly remembered where he had seen Magpie before.

When he was in his 20's he ran cattle in Idaho for a rancher named Dave Hicks. Magpie worked in the kitchen with Dave's wife, Shauna. Ha! What was her name back then? Trudy? Tracy? Stacey!

Brad smiled to himself when he remembered the days on the ranch, partying late and playing cards, flirting with the kitchen girls. Stacy was with someone else in those days, but he thought she was gorgeous. She still was.

He walked to the empty cabin and Magpie followed, curious.

He was smiling like a man with a secret.

"Have you ever lived in Idaho?" he asked her as he opened the door.

"I did, yes."

"Did you ever go to the Panther Creek Hot Springs?" he turned to her in the doorway.

"Oh my God! You have got to be kidding me!" She began to laugh she leaned into the doorjamb.

"That's why you are so familiar! God, we were all like a family there at the ranch. What good memories." She looked him in the face.

Brad turned on the light in the cabin and noticed she was still beautiful. He set the keys on the table and told her she and her daughter could stay as long as they needed.

"Good night," he called as he walked to his truck and drove back to the ranch.

70

Deja & the meaning of life

"Do you want to talk about what happened?" Magpie asked Deja. They were lying in their cots in the 'Bill Monroe' cabin.

"I just want to know why are we even here? Why are we born if we're just going to die?"

"Ah, the meaning of life," Magpie reflected, "the universal question."

"I mean, what am I doing here?"

"I know, honey. What do you think?"

"I've only been around 10 years. I thought you could tell me."

"Deja, you have a gift that goes beyond your years, it is a great responsibility and sometimes a burden."

"I know."

"You didn't have the easiest life before you came to live with me."

"I really miss my mom sometimes."

Magpie heard the tears in her voice. She waited.

"I think Calliope lost her mom, too."

"Yes, she did. She wants to try to find her now."

Deja sighed and turned over, "I'm going to help her."

71

There are some people you can't heal

When Calliope awoke, Cricket was frying bacon and had the atlas spread out on the kitchen table.

"Thanks for cooking breakfast," she said.

"I'm tracing the route we should take to Nevada. Do you still want to go?" Calliope nodded and opened the fridge to get juice while he got the syrup.

"We could leave tomorrow." He looked at her as she grabbed a glass from the open shelf above the stove.

"Okay, let's leave tomorrow," she said with more conviction. "I'll go to the Pub and look up my mom's name in the Rainbow list."

"But Cricket..." she continued. She sat down and looked at the map with him. "I wonder if I should find my Granny first or my mom?"

Their heads were bent over the atlas; his finger traced the route he wanted to take.

"Why don't you look them both up and get the information, then decide?"

"I don't even know if they are still alive," she hesitated at the thought, but it's what they were both thinking anyway.

When they took their breakfast outside to eat, Deja and Juno were playing Frisbee again.

Magpie came out of the cabin with coffee and toast.

"What a beautiful morning! I'm so glad to be here."

"Hey, girlfriend, good morning," Calliope was glad she could visit with her friend for one more day.

"Cricket and I are going to leave tomorrow for Nevada," she announced.

Deja and Juno came to greet Calliope and grab some food.

"Can I go?" Asked Deja. Cricket and Calliope laughed.

"I'm gonna miss you, Deja, but that's a long ways and you and Magpie have to get your bus and go home, too."

"Can I see your cabin?" she asked Calliope.

They grabbed hands and walked to the cabin.

"'Gary Lee Moore Cabin'" she read out loud.

"They all seem to be named after famous fiddlers," commented Calliope.

"Your cabin looks like ours," said Deja. She picked up the <u>Language of Insects</u> book off the table.

"This is the book Cricket wrote, huh?"

"Yep."

"Would he sign a copy for me do you think?"

"Of course he would."

Deja sat at the little table flipping the pages.

"You grew up without a mom, huh?"

"My Granny raised me," she answered.

"I remember my mom," Deja volunteered.

"What do you remember?"

"Well, we used to walk to the park and visit her friends. She had lots of friends. And she would let me fix food for the two of us."

"That sounds like fun," said Calliope.

"But she couldn't take care of us one day and then she didn't like getting up in the morning. I made too much noise and then she would say mean things. Something was wrong with her brain," Deja described as best she could.

"That happens to some people. They don't do it on purpose, honey."

"I know."

Deja saw the Atlas open to Nevada.

"Is that where you lived?"

"Yep."

"And that's where you're going on Wednesday?"

"I hope so."

"Calliope?"

"Yes?"

"Why did Scorpio shoot himself?" Her face twisted and she looked up at the clouds. Tears spilled from her blue eyes.

"Oh, Deja. There are some people you can't heal." She held the little girl tightly and rocked her while she cried. While they both cried.

"I tried to tell him there were people who loved him," she said into Calliope's shoulder.

"I know, I know."

"I hope you find your mom."

"I do too."

72

Magpie & Brad

Magpie was sitting on the sunbench petting Juno and talking to Cricket when Brad's truck pulled up.

"Are you done feeding for the day?" Magpie asked as Brad approached.

"Sit down, Brad, let's catch up! Do you ever see Gary or Mike?"

"Well, look at that little cabin next to yours," he said.

"'Gary Lee Moore Cabin' Ha! You do still keep in touch. I'm of a mind to get out my fiddle right now and play a tune."

Now it was his turn to laugh, "Bring it on out here, I happened to bring my mandolin with me this morning."

"So what about Mike?" she asked when he got back from the truck with his instrument.

"He's living in Thailand with his new wife and family; but he'll be here for the contest. I can't wait to tell those guys I ran into you."

He pulled his mandolin out of the case and pulled the pick out of the strings. He strummed a chord to see if it was still in tune and then looked at Magpie expectantly.

She stood up and went into her cabin and brought out her fiddle case.

"I suppose you are going to pick the first song?" she teased as she flashed her eyes at him.

"Shady Grove," he named and they were off. Oh the memories! Her heart was filled by this simple tune, the one they used to play together in the bunkhouse when all the guys would hang out to play music. It seemed like 'their song'.

"Rabbit Where's Yer Mammy," she called out and off they went again.

Deja and Calliope came outside to see what was going on, and Cricket drew near to watch.

They all clapped when the song was over, but Brad and Magpie were on to the next one. This one they sang in harmony like they knew what they were doing. They did. It was another old favorite they had worked out years ago and neither had ever forgotten.

"Oh, Come, Angel Band,
Come and around me stand;
Oh bear me away on your snowy wings
To my eternal home;
Oh, bear me away on your snowy wings
To my eternal home."

Their voices faded after the end of the song. They were both smiling.

The girls went back into the cabin to look at the map and Cricket lay down in the hammock.

"Brad, this was just the tonic I needed," Magpie said.

"Me too, 'Stacy'."

"Oh, ha!" she slapped him playfully on the shoulder, and leaned close; "don't let anyone hear you call me that, I'll never hear the end of it."

"Well, I like the name Magpie," he declared, "I have a magpie logo for my business."

"No way, let me see it."

He showed her his business card.

"Ha, you weren't kidding me."

She took it from him and tucked it into her blouse.

73

Calliope finds Garcia

Calliope spent most of the day before doing research at the Pub. She took her laptop and set it up at a table near the window.

Calliope went through list after list in the Rainbow Guide looking for her mom's name.

When Patrick came to take her order, he stopped for a minute and said, "Hey, you're Cricket's wife, aren't you?"

"I am."

"Glad to meet you, finally. Cricket is a great guy."

"We're staying out at Brad's fiddle camp."

"I know, he told me."

Patrick heard the phone ring and went to answer it.

Her heart beat faster as she noticed a listing for Garcia. No first or last name.

Patrick brought her food and asked about her project.

"I'm looking at the Rainbow Guide for someone."

"The Rainbow Guide?" he asked.

"Never mind," she pointed to the screen and said, "I just found Garcia, my mom's boyfriend."

"Interesting."

"He lives in the Sheldon Antelope Wildlife Range."

"That's near Denio Junction, down in Nevada," Patrick had been there before.

Calliope continued to stare at the screen. Then she picked up the road atlas and searched for the Antelope Range.

Patrick sat down and pointed to the map.

"Here it is." he said, "You take 395 most of the way..." Calliope pulled a highlighter out of her purse to mark the route. "That will take you about 6 hours."

"Cricket and I can stay in Denio Junction."

She took a bite of her burger and fries and looked at Patrick, "This buffalo burger is good. Did you make the sweet potato fries?"

74

Garcia's not home, man

Calliope never found her mom in the Rainbow listing, but finding Garcia was a good start. She and Cricket got into the car they borrowed from Brad and began their journey.

"I wonder if we should call Garcia ahead, did you find a phone number?" Cricket asked as he punched buttons on the radio.

"No."

"Maybe we can call the park and see if he works there."

"How are you going to call a park?" she snapped.

"You don't have to get crabby."

"Sorry."

"So what about Brad and Magpie? Isn't that a cool thing?" He changed the subject.

"I know," she answered, "I loved hearing them play together. They seemed to hit it off right away."

"Well, they met each other years ago. It will be interesting to see how it all works out when we get back from Nevada," said Cricket.

"I'm half excited and half scared," she admitted. "The listing for Garcia is recent, so I guess he's still in the Park. A visit with him is a good start. He would know the real story, right?"

"We're going to do our best for you, honey," her husband answered and put his hand on hers.

"I have something for you," Cricket said when they had been on the road a few hours.

"What?" She loved presents.

"Look in the glovebox."

She took out a hinged satin box and opened it carefully. It was a gold necklace with a small hornet on the end. It had a diamond set carefully on each of its wings.

"Fiercely Loyal."

"Yes, sweetheart, I'm fiercely loyal to you. I'd do anything to help you get through this."

"Thank you, Cricket."

"No, really, I almost lost you and I want you to know that I want to help you heal and I want to be the one that you can come to when you need to talk."

She began to protest, "I don't know."

"I mean it, Calliope," he put his hand in hers, "There's a reason you don't tell me about your fears… or your dreams. Can we just start over? Are you ever going to trust me?"

Calliope squeezed his hand and put the necklace on. She looked at him and nodded, "I would love to start over."

She looked at the scenery and swallowed her confession.

"I would love to start over," she looked at him and then turned away. "I do trust you," Calliope sighed.

Calliope closed her eyes and leaned her head back and fell asleep.

"Where are we? Was I sleeping?"

"Yes, you've been sleeping about two hours now. We're almost to Canyon City, we'll stop there and get some lunch."

Calliope stretched and rearranged her clothes. How did her clothes get so twisted around just sitting in a car?

"Do you think we will get there before tonight? Or do you want to stay somewhere on the way?" She asked him.

"Let's see what happens when the time comes."

"Okay."

Garcia heard a car approaching. A young couple got out of the car that they had parked near his trailer. Not many people came all the way to his living quarters. He watched as they went to his trailer and knocked. They didn't see him out in the field. Garcia had been observing the grasses and native plants to see if the wild horses in this area affected them.

Garcia saw them go back to their car when he didn't answer the door and they stood by the front bumper. They were talking. They seemed harmless. He was still undecided about whether to talk to them or not.

They got into the car and closed the doors then started the car and left. He continued with his work. They were probably lost. Someone else could help them.

"I thought that was his trailer; I guess he must be out."

Calliope was half relieved no one was home. Maybe her mother lived there if she and Garcia were still together. This was one emotional roller coaster.

She had been having flashbacks, too, more memories of living with her mom and Garcia, the Rainbow people, and also her Granny.

75

He lives at the Antelope Refuge

"What do you want to do now?" Cricket asked his wife.

"Let's find a hotel, there's supposed to be one in Denio Junction. We might be able to ask around about Garcia. I wonder if my mom lives there?"

"Maybe," Cricket said.

"I remember that my mom said to watch out for Granny. I think we were hiding from her."

Cricket listened to her and nodded, he wanted to encourage her to remember everything.

"She was so nice, though," Calliope said.

"Did she ever give you an explanation as to why you were living with her instead of your mom?"

"She would change the subject. She didn't want to talk about it."

"Was she good to you?"

"She tried to be a mom for me," Calliope paused for a moment before continuing. "She taught me everything I needed to know to get along in this world. "

"When was the last time you saw her?"

"I left for college and never went back home. That's when we met. Remember, I was working at that bar and living with the guys from the restaurant?"

He nodded and asked, "I wonder who that man was that came to your gate that day?"

"I assumed it was a representative from Child Protection."

He set his right arm across her shoulders as he drove, "Let's see if we can talk to Garcia, I know he can tell us the story."

They arrived in Denio Junction and had a look around. It was a very small town. Cricket didn't think there were any smaller towns than Utopia, but this town only had a gas station, a bar, a motel and a small grocery store. 'Nevada Rockhounds Meet tonight 7:00' said the flier on the store window.

"Can we get a room for a few nights?" Cricket asked the girl at the front desk.

"Fill this out," she pushed a card toward him across the counter.

The girl was watching Judge Judy and looking at her phone; she obviously had more important things to do.

"Do you know a guy named Garcia?"

"No," she looked up from her phone and back down again.

"Okay, then, do you know the guy that works at the Antelope Refuge?"

"Anthony? Yeah." That got her attention for some reason.

"Can you tell me anything about him?"

"Why?"

"We need to see him," Cricket didn't have to explain anything to this girl.

"He lives at the Antelope Refuge."

"And?"

"He comes to town once a week for the Rockhound meeting."

"Thank you." Finally, some information.

"You're in room 3." She slid the key toward him and looked back down at her phone. She was probably texting their whole conversation to her friends. Jeez.

Cricket found Calliope at the little store next door studying the dates on the cans of food.

"What do you want to pick up for snacks?"

"How about some smoked almonds and a six-pack?"

She added these to her basket and they made their way to the check-stand. This place was cool; it had everything from jewelry to travel scrabble. She grabbed some postcards when they were at the counter.

"How're you folks today?" said the gal behind the counter.

"Just drove all day from up near Pendleton," said Cricket.

"That's a long ways," she commented.

"We'll be staying in the motel for a few nights."

"What brings you to Denio?"

"We're interested in the Antelope Range," Calliope answered.

"You ain't one of them environmentalists are ya?"

"No, we want to visit with the caretaker."

"Anthony?"

"Yes, yes, Anthony," said Calliope. "We went by his place but he wasn't there."

"He's usually out in the park somewhere all day. He hangs out with the animals, mostly."

The couple looked at each other.

"Do you know him?"

"We all know each other around here, not a lot of people to choose from." The gal was beginning to hold back a little. She was suspicious of outsiders. She didn't know if she was comfortable telling them anything else.

"Has he lived around here very long?" Calliope asked anxiously.

"Depends on what you mean by long," she answered warily.

They were getting nowhere this way; she had shut them out for some reason.

"Never mind. See ya later." The couple left the store and Shirley called out to Anthony's place and left a message on his phone.

"What do you want to do, now?" Cricket asked her.

"I wish you would quit asking me that," Calliope snapped.

"Sorry."

She looked out the window of the motel, then walked across the room and sat on the bed.

"No, I'm sorry. I can't help it, I'm just stressed out..."

He sat next to her and wrapped his arms around her, "It's okay," he said quietly in her ear.

He held both her hands in his, "Calliope... Angeline, we're in this together. Do you still want to be with me?"

"Of course," she said uncertainly.

76

At Garcia's place

"I guess we could attend the Rockhounds meeting tonight," Cricket suggested.

"Okay. I'm sorry, my memories are so strong it's as if I wasn't even here. This is freaking me out."

"Well, you're safe here in the motel with me, honey. It's natural to be anxious, this is a very courageous step you're taking."

Calliope was jiggling her knee and biting her fingers at the same time. Cricket brought a chair from the other side of the table and sat next to her. He got her attention and gently took her hand in his, "You can stop any time. We can go home whenever you say."

"I know. Thank you Cricket. There's no way around this, it's got to be done."

Anthony pulled into the parking lot of the bar in his 1980 Jeep Cherokee Wagon and slid across the seat. He opened the passenger side door and climbed out. The driver's door hadn't worked since 2001.

Calliope and Cricket were watching through the motel window. The two burst through door number 3 to catch him before he entered the bar for the meeting.

"Garcia?" asked Calliope.

"Yes?" He was expecting the intrusion; his friend had called him from the store a little while ago.

Her throat was closing up and she felt like she would choke.

"My name is Angeline Sweetwater."

Calliope stood with her hands clasped in front of her like a child as she waited for him to react. Would Garcia remember her?

She could tell he was caught by surprise. He stared at her. Then she watched the recognition dawn on his face.

Garcia came to her and took her by the shoulders with both hands. "Oh, Angeline, you have grown into a beautiful young woman. I am very glad to see you." He grabbed her in a hug.

He turned to Cricket who introduced himself and they shook hands.

"How on earth did you find me?" he asked.

"You're in the Rainbow guide. Thank goodness you still go by Garcia. I didn't know your real name."

"You can still call me Garcia," he answered. "Come on, why don't you follow me to my place and we can have a proper reunion?" Calliope and Cricket agreed and they all set out for his place.

Everyone settled in the living room of the caretaker's trailer at the Antelope Refuge. The three of them trying to catch up, but still feeling a little awkward.

Cricket popped a beer from the six-pack he brought, and offered one to Garcia who declined, "I don't drink, man," he explained. But he offered the couple some weed.

"So, Garcia, I've come because I need to know what happened that day Granny took me home with her. I never knew what happened. I still don't know where my mom is."

Garcia put his pipe on the coffee table and sat forward. The couch was covered with a batik throw; he had a wall hanging of Ganesh on a blue background behind the couch.

"Can you help me?" Calliope asked.

"Angeline, you were the light of your mother's life. And mine."

"I changed my name to Calliope," she interrupted him. It seemed important somehow.

"Ah, child of Zeus, the thunder god."

Cricket kept to himself in the recliner.

Garcia took another hit off the pipe and set it down before he spoke again.

"Your Grandmother did not think we were raising you in the most optimum of circumstances. She spent just as much time tracking us down as we spent hiding from her. We were Rainbows. We camped with each other all over the country. Granny thought you should have a formal education, that you needed stability, a house and a neighborhood. The whole fucking establishment, man." He grabbed the pipe again. This whole thing was making him nervous. Garcia inhaled seemingly forever.

"I got a prescription for this," he held up his carved antler pipe.

Calliope continued to wait for the rest of the story.

"Do you want something to drink? Soda?"

"No, thank you," she answered.

"So, your mom. Well, anyway, she had some bad times. Like she would get caught up in paranoia and shit. Then she would take pills or do anything to feel better. She had an addictive personality. I mean, Wow."

"When I got to Granny's I wrote you guys a letter, did you get it?"

"Umm, yeah. We made a few phone calls and we were going to go up to your Granny's house." His voice faded as he bent down to take off his shoes.

"Then your mom got really sick and I had to get her to the hospital."

"You guys were coming for me?"

"Yeah, we really were. But your mom had some serious withdrawals from heroin and I had to drop her off. She was in the hospital for a couple weeks. I hung out in town while she got off the smack and then we went back to the forest. God, I loved that tree house," Garcia added to himself.

"Your mom called your Granny to try to get you back, but she had found out about the hospital and said she'd take us to court. So we let you go. It was really devastating for the both of us, but we knew it was the best thing for you."

He grabbed a leather lace from the table and tied his hair back.

"Didn't you go to school and shit?"

"Well, yes, but couldn't you guys visit or something?"

"We were always going to, but we couldn't pull it off."

Calliope felt like she was 12 again.

"Do you know where my mom is now?" Calliope asked.

"Honey, she died three years ago. I'm so sorry."

77

You know these guys?

Calliope slumped like she had been punched in the stomach. She felt sick and dizzy at once.

"Can you tell me what happened?" she asked when she found her voice.

"Well, me and your mom weren't together anymore," he draped his elbows on his knees.

"She left me for some dude she met at a gathering, free love and all that. We had been split up for, like, seven years. She and that guy had a kid, but they didn't stay together either. I lost track of them for a while," he had a faraway look on his face while he reminisced.

"The last time I saw your mom was at a gathering three years ago, which was a trip, because she didn't go to the gatherings any more. But here she was in Missoula. She had her beautiful girl with her. She seemed in worse shape than ever."

"Hey, you guys want some apples? I got a whole box of apples yesterday from a friend of mine in Washington."

"Garcia, please tell me the rest of the story."

"Okay, so, she looked strung out again and next thing I knew, she had left. Just vanished. No one saw her but she left her little girl behind with a friend of hers at the gathering. Her daughter was like 7. She went home with this gal and lived with her. I think she still lives with her. But your mom died of an overdose three years ago."

He looked down, avoiding Calliope's eyes. He nervously fiddled with the items on the coffee table. Rolling scraps of paper into tubes, arranging and rearranging them into patterns while he talked.

Calliope was biting her lip. She looked at Cricket who was in the recliner listening to the story. Heroin overdose, God.

"I don't really remember my mom being like that. Heroin? Really?"

"Well, we weren't exactly Ozzie and Harriett," he picked at his cuticles to avoid her eyes.

She straightened up in her chair. She had a sister.

"So, can you tell me anything about my sister? Do you know her name or where she lives? How old would she be now, about 10?"

"I have a picture somewhere," he went to the bookcase and rummaged through a stack of papers and CD's. He held one up, "You want to listen to some Modest Mouse?" he asked. He went to the CD player and loaded it up and turned it on. He turned back to the couch to sit down.

"The photo?" Calliope reminded him.

"Oh, it's over here somewhere," he picked up the stack again and sorted through it.

"Here it is, you can have this picture," he handed the photo to her and then sat on the couch, relieved to have something to give her.

She was looking at a photo of Magpie and Deja.

Cricket was curious about the photo and got out of the recliner when he saw his wife's reaction. She pointed at the picture and let out a cry. She held her hand over her mouth and held the photo up for Cricket to see. Garcia had loaded his pipe and was looking for matches when he heard her cry out.

"This is Magpie and Deja! Deja is my sister? Are you sure this is the right picture?"

He got up and took it from her, "Yeah, man, you know Magpie and Deja?"

The couple was stunned. Calliope was torn between taking the photo and leaving right then and there or staying and pumping him for information, she wanted to pick his fuzzy headed cloudy little brain.

"I just met them at the Barter Faire in Utopia," she told him.

"I been there," he said, "the fairy congress is awesome. Hey, you guys want to see my chickens?'

"We better get going," Cricket made the decision for the both of them, "We'll come back tomorrow. Can we get your phone number?"

Garcia wrote his number on the back of a Christmas card after a confusing search for a pen. "Hey, come back again, I'd like to talk about old times." He called to them from the porch as they got into their car. They backed out of the driveway as Garcia stood in the doorway watching.

78

Calliope's new dream

"Did we just visit with a stoner in a little trailer who told us your mom died of a heroin overdose or did I dream that?" Cricket was still trying to process the last hour.

"God, I know. I'm trying to piece together the story from my memory as a kid, and I can see how that makes sense."

"Really? Isn't it weird how we grow up a certain way and we think it's normal?" her husband commented, "What kind of things are you remembering?"

"When we went to the gatherings, we would stay in the 'Kid's Camp' with some of the mothers. We had our own things to do, nature hikes and making birdhouses and stuff. But I didn't see much of my mom while we were there."

"That doesn't prove that she was an addict."

"There were lots of times when I couldn't get mom to wake up. It would scare me, but Garcia was always there to take care of us. He would take care of me and we would go to the little grocery together. She would be in her own world. I never saw any needles or anything."

"I guess Garcia was covering for her and you wouldn't notice really," Cricket commented.

"I forgot to ask him if he knew anything about my Granny. She might still be alive."

"We can call him tomorrow."

"I really want to call Magpie right now - OH MY GOD, that makes Magpie friends with my mom! She would know my mom better than anyone." She jumped up from where she was sitting on the edge of the bed and paced, holding the photo.

"Deja is my SISTER! This is too much," she spun around and grabbed Cricket in a hug. "I don't even know what to do next!" her mind was in a spin.

"We can't call Magpie, the cabins don't have phones. Does she have a cell phone?" Asked Cricket.

"I don't know. If she does I don't have the number. Do you know Brad's number?"

"No, I don't have his number. Honey, let's sit on this for tonight and call them in the morning. We've got a lot to think about."

"Oh, but that means Deja's mom is dead, too. Jeez, this is getting crazy!"

He let his wife chatter, it would do her good to talk and talk until she had it all straight. He took his shoes off and lay on top of the covers, stacking all the pillows behind him. He arranged both hands behind his head and settled in for the duration.

Cricket woke up in the same position he had been in when he fell asleep listening to his wife. The light was off and she lay beside him curled up to sleep. God; she really needed the rest. This was a mind-blowing revelation. He knew they were in for a crazy day tomorrow, but what was he thinking, life was going to be crazy for a long time.

Cricket got up and went looking for coffee before his wife woke up. He found some at the little grocery next door, where he also bumped into the same gal as the day before.

"How's it going?" she asked.

"I think I just need some coffee."

"Did you find Anthony?"

"Yeah, we did."

She was waiting for him to fill her in, but neither of them said anything. He filled two cups from the pumper pots at the 'Koffee Kounter', paid for his coffee and left.

He heard the phone ringing as he got to their door but Calliope answered it before he came into the room.

"Good Morning to you, too," she was saying.

"Well, let me ask Cricket and get back to you. Okay, talk to you later."

She hung up and looked at him.

"God what a night! I had the weirdest dreams. You wanna hear this? It's crazy."

Cricket was nodding his head, not even trying to get a word in edgewise.

"I was at that gas station, remember my recurring dream? I was there again and there were people all over, the bus pulled in and there was a big party. Lots of foods, lots of people, like everyone I knew. Somehow we owned the gas station, but we didn't. The displays were filled with food and colorful gifts.

And it was filled with ladybugs. They were flying and they were landing on the bus and on the people. We were laughing."

"That's so cool, honey."

"I think that's a good sign, don't you?" She got dressed and was brushing her hair as she spoke. She paused and looked at him from the mirror.

"I do, yes."

"The silverfish are all gone, I see ladybugs all over. I always wanted my life to be like ladybugs. You know, good luck."

"Jeez, what was that thing with Garcia? Holy Cow, right?" He brought up.

"He just called to see if we wanted to meet up today."

"This is your gig, Calliope. Whatever you want to do."

"I think as long as we're here, let's see what else he has to say. I'll call him back and tell him we'll meet for breakfast at the bar."

Calliope punched in his number on her cell.

79

She never stopped looking for you

"Sorry again about your mom, Angel, I mean Calliope." Garcia came into the café and was setting a bag on the table where they sat.

Calliope stood up for a hug and Cricket held out his hand for a friendly shake. They were really curious about what he would say today. This guy was not only an unusual character; he was a wealth of information.

"I got some stuff in here for you guys," Garcia proceeded to take things out of the bag.

"Here's some of those apples I was telling you about," he took them out one by one and laid them on the table. Garcia handed one to Calliope and one to Cricket like they were gold. Then he sat down and put the bag on the floor and continued to pull things out. He handed her a sketchbook, which she opened and exclaimed, "I remember drawing these!"

Cricket slid his chair next to her and looked over her shoulder, "Those are cool, Calliope."

She came to a sketch that she had made of her mother and it brought tears to her eyes. Calliope couldn't remember what her mom looked like, but this reminded her of how she looked in her heart.

Garcia handed her a carved wooden stash box. In it was a tiny book with a silver lock and key, a matchbox, a magpie feather, and a tooth. She cradled the tiny book in her hands, "My diary." Calliope began to open the pages, but decided to look at it later, in private. She handled all the items, opening the matchbox and finding dried flower petals.

Calliope set the items aside, waiting to see what else was in the bag.

"Can I bring you anything to drink?" The waitress appeared at the table.

She took their drink orders and set down the silverware rolled in a napkin, and poured water.

"Missed you at the meeting last night, Anthony," she mentioned to Garcia. "We saw a great snowflake obsidian that Shorty brought in."

"I'll be there next time," he said.

"So, I gotta know about Magpie and Deja. You know them?" Anthony asked after the waitress walked away.

"Well, I followed her bus to the Barter Faire. Was that just a week ago?" Calliope looked at Cricket who nodded.

"Starry Night. Awesome bus, man. We all had a hand in that work of art." Garcia was smiling at the memory.

"So, I stopped at their camp that day to be friendly and we hit it off right away. And Deja is a doll; she has such energy."

"She's a healer, that girl," he added.

"I know, she actually worked in the healing tent last weekend. She knows just the right thing to say."

"God, I can't believe that she's my sister. It's so weird." Calliope stopped suddenly and looked at Garcia. "You are absolutely sure that my mother is her mother?"

"Yes." He held up his hand to swear.

The waitress came back to their table and had pen to paper, ready to take their order. They hadn't even looked at their menus yet, but Garcia told them he wanted the Grandpa Special. Calliope didn't know if she could even eat, but asked for the same. Cricket wanted biscuits and gravy.

After they ordered, she leaned across the table toward him, "Do you know anything about my Grandma?"

"I know that she loved you so much that she never stopped looking for you."

80

The memory box

Tears welled in her eyes and dripped onto the cover of the sketchpad. Calliope didn't bother wiping them; she didn't even notice she was crying. She suddenly wanted to see her Granny more than anything.

"Do you think she still lives in the same place?"

"I don't know much about her, Angel. I've been on the antelope preserve for the last five years." Garcia watched the waitress coming to their table with their plates.

Calliope moved her food around her plate. She sipped at her juice absentmindedly.

"Okay, here's some more stuff," Garcia got into the bag and pulled out a rabbit skin and handed it to her.

"We spent a lot of time together, Angel. Remember going to the river and looking for caddisflies?"

"I do, yes. What about the time we found the little bird and I tried to feed it worms and bugs?"

They spent some time reminiscing while Cricket learned more about his wife's childhood. She seemed happier and more animated than he had ever seen her. It was like she was coming to life before his eyes.

The time flew by. Their breakfast was done and it was time to leave. Garcia reached into the bottom of the bag for the last item. He handed Calliope a shoebox. She opened the lid and found photos and notes and other treasures.

"I don't know why I kept this stuff," there were tears in his eyes, now. "I don't need it. You should have it." Garcia held out the empty bag and Cricket took it from him. Cricket began to place the things from the table into the bag while Calliope looked into the box. She looked back up at Garcia and was shaking her head in wonder.

"Garcia, this means the world to me. Thank you for taking care of me all those years ago."

"It was a pleasure," he responded and they embraced warmly. Calliope began to sob into his shoulder and he held her tighter. He had his chin up and his eyes closed, face filled with sorrow and joy at the same time.

What a trip, man.

81

Meanwhile back at the ranch

Brad woke up to the best morning of his life. He had never actually slept in one of the fiddle cabins before, but now seemed a good time to start.

Magpie rolled over and pressed her warm body against his; Brad nuzzled his face into her sweet curls and kissed her ear.

"I've been waiting all my life for this," he whispered.

"Mmmm. Me, too." Magpie felt like this was the beginning of a new life.

Brad tore himself away from her embrace reluctantly and got dressed. It was time to tend to cows and horses. The rising sun cast a light through the window onto the bed, and Brad watched Magpie sleeping on the pile of pillows. He loved the way Magpie's face looked in the morning sunlight.

"I'll be back." Brad kissed her soft cheek and she slept.

Later that morning; Magpie woke to the sound of Deja in the kitchen. Deja had wanted to sleep in the 'Gary Lee Moore' cabin all by herself. Deja missed Calliope, and was taking care of Juno for her.

Deja was cooking some oatmeal for breakfast.

"Hey, Deja," Magpie called into the kitchen.

"Hey, Magpie," Deja called back.

"I'll be right out, honey." She sat up in the bed and pulled her dress over her head.

Deja was filling the coffee reservoir with water.

"Magpie?" Deja called from the kitchen.

She came walking in from the bedroom, "Yes?"

"I hope Calliope finds her mom."

She hugged Deja, "I do, too."

"Let's not leave just yet," Deja said.

"Good idea," Magpie replied. "We can't go until they release our bus, anyway."

"Wow, listen to all the birds," Deja opened the door so she could listen to the morning chorus.

Magpie stretched and got a cup from the shelf.

"How was your night, sleeping in your own little place?"

"I loved it," declared Deja. Juno blasted in the door, looking for breakfast.

"We can't leave yet, anyway," said Magpie, "not until after the Fiddle Contest."

"Juno Juno Juno Juno!" sang Deja. She ran in a circle and then out the door. The pup followed, hind end swinging with joy, knocking into the table on the way out and sloshing the juice. Deja filled the dog dish and then ran back up the step into the cabin.

"Do you love Brad?" She asked as she popped her head in the door.

"Oh God, I might," Magpie said this with surprise. She hadn't been in love for a long, long time. She didn't realize how much she had thought of him all these years. Magpie had been attracted to him back then, but they only flirted with each other. She was attached to another guy back then. She hardly remembered him. What if she had stayed and hooked up with Brad instead of leaving? What would her life have been like?

"-I said, can we go to town today and get some more food for Juno?" Deja was patting her on the arm.

"Yes, let's go to town. No, wait, we can't. We don't have any way to get there. Brad will be back later, he can drive us."

"My birthday is next week. I'm gonna be 11," Deja declared.

"I know. What do you want?"

"I'm not sure yet, I'll make a list today."

"I bet you will," predicted Magpie.

Deja ran off to find paper and pencil in the cabin.

After breakfast, they heard Brad pull into the driveway.

Magpie waited on the porch while he got out of the truck and walked toward her. He had two bouquets of flowers and he handed one to Deja as she ran up to him in greeting.

"My very own flowers!" She hugged him and ran to get a container and some water. Brad slid his arm around Magpie and handed her the other bouquet.

"I love wildflowers," she took them and kissed him.

"You still like me?" He asked.

She nodded and looked up at him, "I'm happy to see you."

Juno ran up to them with the Frisbee, wanting them to throw it.

"Do you girls want to come up to the ranch this afternoon?"

"I think you could talk us into that. Hey, we need to get to the store sometime today, can you take us?"

"Sure."

Deja came out with a piece of paper, "I made a list!"

"Give it here," said Magpie and Deja handed her the list.

"Ahh, jewelry. What kind?"

"I really love the turquoise beaded jewelry we saw at the Barter Faire this weekend."

"Let's see, new sandals and a dress. And a diary. Very interesting list."

"I can make a cake," said Brad.

They both looked at him. "Really, I can bake."

"Well, why not?" Magpie couldn't stop smiling.

"Are we having a party?" Deja was trying to stand on one leg as long as she could.

"We are having a party!"

"Juno, a party! I'm going to be 11!" They began to run across the field to the stage. When they got there, she jumped up on the stage and Juno followed. They did a dance and she sang a quick song at the top of her lungs, and then they ran down again.

"Deja is a wonderful girl," Brad commented as they sat down to the picnic table.

"She's been living with me for over three years."

"Where's her mother?" He asked.

"She was having some problems and came to me one day and asked if I could take care of her daughter." Magpie said carefully.

"Really? What kind of problems? Or is that too personal?"

"I don't mind telling you. She had a problem with heroin, Deja doesn't know the specifics, but she knows that her mom had problems. I don't keep much from her. She used to have to take care of her mom. I love Deja."

"Where is her mom now?"

"We don't know. We never saw her again."

"Do you want some oatmeal? Deja made it."

They ate breakfast outside and then Magpie went to their cabin and got her fiddle and began to tune it.

"Have you got anything more important to do right now?" she asked.

"Not a thing," he answered, and went to the cabin and brought out his mandolin.

82

Meanwhile back at the other ranch

Later that afternoon they were at Brad's, helping him with the animals on the ranch. He showed them the barn and introduced them to the horses.

"You ever ride a horse?"

"I have," said Magpie.

"No," said Deja, thinking this needed to change today.

Brad opened the stall door and brought out his bay mare.

"This is Sugar," he announced and the girls began to pet her and talk to her. She was loving it.

"Am I going to ride her?" Deja asked.

"Yep." Brad walked her to the hitching post with the lead rope and hiked Deja onto the old mare's back.

She was in heaven. This was the best thing she had ever done. This is what Deja wanted to do for the rest of her life. She would ride and ride and never get off.

Magpie waited at the barn while Brad led Deja around the field. She could see they were talking as they went. Magpie was falling hard and fast for this guy.

83

Cricket & Calliope home again

It was dark and Deja was in bed when Cricket and Calliope pulled into the driveway. Juno was lying on the porch step and sat up when she heard the car. Calliope laughed when she noticed her new collar; pink with sparkles.

They didn't even unload the car. Calliope carried a box with her to Magpie's cabin door and knocked.

Calliope and Cricket were greeted with warm hugs when Magpie answered the door. Brad was sitting at the kitchen table. A bottle of wine sat on the table and the radio was on.

"I'm so glad to see you!" Magpie said, "Sit down and tell us all about your trip."

"Magpie, this was such an intense trip." Calliope set the box on the floor and sat down at the table.

"You are not going to believe what happened while we were there. Oh, I'm so tired! And hungry," she interrupted herself and grabbed some grapes from the fruit bowl.

Magpie jumped up and opened the fridge. Getting out the leftovers, she set them on a plate for the couple. Ribs, garlic bread, watermelon.

Calliope talked while she and Cricket picked food off the plate.

"Okay," Calliope began, "so we met Garcia. He lives on the Antelope Preserve. We stayed in Denio Junction at a motel. We went to his trailer to meet up with him the first time, and then we had breakfast with him this morning," she sounded like a newspaper reporter.

Magpie tried to be patient and wait for the story.

"Where's Deja?" Calliope asked suddenly.

"She wanted to sleep in your cabin so she could see you first thing when you got here."

"Okay, good."

Magpie was looking at the box.

Calliope had been thinking about this all day, and still didn't know how to tell the story. She just opened the box and handed Magpie the photo of her mom that had been sitting on top of the photos. It was a beautiful woman who looked a lot like Calliope. She was standing in the trees, sunlight slanting down on her. Her mother held Calliope in her arms. They were looking at each other and laughing.

Magpie took the picture from her friend and gasped. She held her hand over her mouth, her eyes wide.

"Junie is your mother?"

Calliope nodded, her eyes bright with tears.

"Where is she? Did he know?"

She paused and said quietly, "She died of a heroin overdose."

Magpie got up. So did Calliope. They embraced and rocked each other in their grief. The guys made a silent exit out the cabin door. They knew the two women wouldn't miss them.

"That's intense," said Brad when they got outside.

"You haven't heard the half of it," Cricket replied.

"What else happened?"

"Deja and Calliope are sisters," he watched Brad's face as he relayed the news.

"That's a trip."

He told Brad the whole story as they sat outside watching the moon rise. They could see the girls at the table through the window in the glow of the kitchen light.

"So what are you guys going to do?"

"We're moving to Utopia. I hope Magpie decides to stay, too."

"So do I," said Brad.

It was late when the couple decided to call it a night. They got their suitcases from the car and brought them into the cabin. Deja never even stirred in her sleep. She slept in a pile of blankets on the floor where she had settled in for the night. Cricket and Calliope got into bed and fell asleep immediately.

84

Deja finds a photo

"Why do you have a picture of my mom?" Deja was patting Calliope on the arm to wake her up. She couldn't wait another minute. Deja had found it on the kitchen table in a box. She had to wake Calliope and find out.

The woman awoke and quickly got out of bed, she didn't want to wake Cricket. Calliope put her arm around Deja and led her into the kitchen. Deja had opened the box, thinking it was a birthday present.

She held out the picture to Calliope, "How did you get this picture of my mom? Do you know her?" There was excitement in her voice.

"I do, Deja. Let's go outside."

Juno was waiting on the steps for her breakfast, Deja obliged.

Calliope went in and got one of the blankets off the floor and brought it out. She sat in the hammock and waited for Deja.

The little girl sat down next to Calliope and they lay in the hammock together, tucked into the blanket. They were looking at the morning sky through the tops of the trees. Deja was looking at the picture as they swung gently back and forth.

"Is that me in the picture?"

Calliope sighed, "Actually, that's me," she said.

Deja searched her brain trying to figure it out.

"How could you be that baby? I mean, why is my mom holding you? Did my mom know you when you were a baby?"

The hammock continued to rock gently while Deja sorted it out. Calliope didn't know how else to do this. She waited for the revelation.

Deja held the picture to her heart and she took a deep breath.

"Oh, Calliope," she let out her breath, her eyes closed. She turned her head to look at her sister. Calliope was nodding her head and smiling.

"Does that mean you found your mother? Our mother?" Deja asked excitedly.

"Well, I found mom's boyfriend. His name was Garcia and he told me everything. That's how I found out about you. Look." She pulled the picture of Magpie and Deja from her robe pocket and handed it to Deja.

"That's me and Magpie!" Then she remembered that day. Deja was only seven, but that didn't mean she didn't remember it. The day her mother walked away.

"Do you know why she left me? Do you know where she is?" That's when Deja began to cry. Her little voice cracked and she buried her face into Calliope's neck. They rocked in the hammock, Calliope was crying, too. Her mom had left her, but she had also left Deja. Calliope was angry. She felt lost in the world.

Calliope still hadn't told Deja the rest of the story.

"Deja," Calliope began when she stopped crying, "Our mama was a wounded soul. You know what that's like."

"I do."

"She tried to feel better when she was hurting. No one could help her, and she had many friends if you remember." "We had lots of friends. We went to Rainbow camp and had a good time," said Deja.

"Your mama loved you more than anything. She told Magpie that since the day you were born."

"We've known Magpie a long time."

"When your mama was hurting so badly, she had to go to the hospital. You told me one time that you had to call the ambulance for your mother."

"I did," said Deja gravely.

"Well, she knew she couldn't take care of you anymore so she let Magpie take care of you. Mom knew she could trust Magpie to take care of you and love you until she could come back."

"Is she coming back?" Deja asked hopefully.

"No, she's not, honey." Calliope turned to her little sister, "Garcia told me that our mama died."

"Oh, Calliope, I can't take this," she covered Calliope's mouth, " This is too hard. Don't tell me any more."

"I know. I know," she whispered into Deja's ear as they lay in the hammock together and wept.

85

The Fiddle Contest

The day of the fiddle contest had finally arrived. Magpie, Calliope and Deja, had set up and organized everything. Many guests had come the night before. Music had been going on until all hours, and a bonfire surrounded by jamming musicians.

Calliope and Cricket drove over from their place down the road. They had found a rental house and Calliope had already set up a new tattoo studio in town.

Magpie and Deja were living in the little 'Bill Monroe' cabin and loving it. Brad wanted them to move out to his place, but they were content to stay at the fiddle camp for now. The Starry Night bus was parked at the ranch. It had been detailed and the windshield replaced.

The girls loved meeting Pat, a friend of Brad's for many years. She had such a kind heart and they thought of her as one of them right away. Pat was in charge of the front gate while Magpie made sure the contestants filled out their forms. They were expecting about forty participants and an audience of four hundred.

Cricket was decked out in his lab coat, all the equipment he would need was behind the stage. Compound microscope, measuring utensils, tweezers, nets, and ID book. The winner was going to be awarded a hot air balloon ride, so the competition was fierce.

Brad told them that the Giant Insect contest usually attracted about one hundred entries. It was for kids twelve and under, and they all got a goodie bag as they walked off the stage.

"There's going to be a lot of grasshoppers, I'm afraid." Brad told Cricket, "That's the last minute kids who still want a prize."

"I'm looking forward to it," he responded as Brad took off again to help with a parking problem.

With his 'Insect Judge' name tag, lab coat and safari hat, Cricket was on the job. He had his collection on display and a box of his own books, *The Language of Insects*. They were set up for sale at the t-shirt table, and later he would autograph them for the contest goers.

Calliope had helped Cricket set up a booth last night on the campgrounds near the lunch grill, between the apple cider booth and a taco truck.

His stall was a popular place already. People were looking at his book and talking about insects. Cricket signed several copies and talked about his life's passion.

The judges and tabulator were receiving gift baskets from Deja who enjoyed putting them together the night before. One of the judges had a girl her age and they ran around taking care of the things that needed to be done at the last minute.

The emcee was up checking the microphone and telling people it was about time to start the peewee division, an audience favorite.

"My name is Gary Lee and I'll be entertaining you today in between contestants. This is my tenth year as emcee and I can't wait to get started, so take your seats and we'll call our first little fiddler up to the stage."

The contestants wowed the audience one by one, and the morning passed without a hitch.

Finally it was noon, and the Giant Insect Contest was ready to begin. Cricket took his place at center stage where the volunteers had set up a long table and all the tools needed to measure the insects. Gary continued to emcee, announcing names and insects as they arrived. He would call out the measurements and grams when the assistant passed the slips of paper to him. Cricket was in his moment. This was the best thing he had ever done.

The children were lined up with their containers, waiting for their turn in front of the Insect Judge. They carried coffee cans, yogurt containers, and tiny terrariums in all shapes and sizes.

When Emmett Bondi had his turn, he set his coffee can on the table and carefully opened the lid. Both the judge and his assistant leapt up as the can fell on its side and a handful of tree frogs jumped out.

Emmett scrambled to grab his frogs and stuff them back into the can, and the judges laughed along with the audience.

"You've got yourself some pretty big insects, there," Cricket said as he scooped up a frog from under his chair.

Next came a contestant with a matchbox. When he opened it, he proudly displayed his entry.

"A praying mantis! What a beauty! Do you know the praying mantis is the symbol for Spiritual Power? The Praying Mantis is also the state insect of Connecticut."

"Yow! Ouch!" The kids laughed as the mantis bit the judge.

"That's 25 extra points," the assistant pointed out.

The kids loved him; especially that his name was Cricket.

He saw the shy pill bug, a dead wasp, and someone brought a tomato hornworm. "Eww," said the crowd when he pulled from the cottage cheese container and suspended it from his fingers. "I am not exactly fond of tomato hornworms, myself," he told the kids gathered around.

All the kids had their turn in front of the Insect Judge and then it was time for the final decision. He and his assistant had their heads together, looking over the statistics.

"This one has all its legs, and is from the Pacific Northwest, that gives it 20 points. It also seems to be the biggest. It bit me. Did it bite you?"

"I didn't let it, but it wanted to," his assistant added.

"It is a beauty," they were trying to decide between the Japanese beetle and a huge dragonfly.

"What's your final vote?" Cricket asked him.

"I say dragonfly," he agreed with the entomologist.

"We have a final decision. The judge has made a decision," Gary Lee was announcing through the microphone when they handed him the paper.

"Hey, hey now!" Gary Lee jumped around and waved the paper in the air. Everyone laughed as a yellow jacket dive-bombed the emcee.

The kids gathered around, Little Petey Larson had on his beekeepers helmet with face-net for good luck.

"The first place winner of the hot air balloon ride this year is...Petey Larson and his giant dragonfly!" Everyone cheered for little Pete who kept his helmet on for the presentation of the hot air balloon certificate and replica of a statue of liberty.

The kids were cleared off the stage and things were being set up for the afternoon rounds. The fiddle judges were milling about, eating from the taco truck and talking to old friends.

86

On stage surprise

Brad got on the stage and took hold of the microphone.

"Before we start the second half of the contest, Magpie and I have some special songs we want to play for you," he announced.

Magpie came up to the stage with her fiddle. Brad took his mandolin out of the tweed case. Mike Oenbring and his daughter Anna came up the stairs from the other side, along with Rod Anderson, the tireless accompanist.

They played a set of four songs with Magpie singing boisterously. The audience loved it.

Brad tapped Magpie on the shoulder and motioned for her to come to the center of the stage with him. That's when Mike and Anna began to play a waltz. Brad took Magpie's hands and began to waltz with her on the stage. She was a little confused by it, but danced good-naturedly with her sweetheart.

He stopped and took the microphone in one hand and Magpie's hand in the other and spoke to the audience.

"This is Magpie, whom I've known for many years. A long time ago, we spent time together as friends and when she moved away, I realized I should have never let her go. She never knew how I felt about her back then, but I've loved her all my life," Brad turned to Magpie who couldn't wipe the smile off her face.

"Now you know how I feel about you," he said. She nodded.

Brad knelt before Magpie and opened a box that held an engagement ring and said, "Magpie, will you marry me?"

"I don't know, let me see the ring," she said. Brad held it up for her to take it from the box. She held it up to the light and then looked back down at him, enjoying the moment.

"Okay, I'll do it!" she finally answered.

The crowd cheered and whistled and hollered as he slipped the ring onto her finger.

Mike and Anna and Rod broke into a rousing rendition of "Shove the Pig's Foot a Little Closer to the Fire" as Magpie and Brad did the two-step on stage. Other couples jumped on the stage and danced along in this unexpected change in the proceedings.

87

Evening camp

The camp that evening was filled with tents and fire barrels and musicians. Cricket was holding court near the 'Kimber Ludiker' cabin. The budding entomologists were gathered around his small table Cricket had set it up with his treasured collection of insects from around the world.

"This doesn't mean I'm moving out of my little 'Gary Lee Moore' cabin, I hope you know," Magpie told Brad.

"Well, I could move in there," he answered.

"Oh no, you don't," she held up her hand and laughed. "I love my little cabin just the way it is."

"Besides," she added, "I believe in long engagements."

Brad looked at Deja for help.

"Don't look at me," Deja said, "I'm planning to hang out at your barn with Sugar."

She ran off with her new fiddle to join the rest of the kids that were jamming on the other side of the stage. Only eighteen and younger allowed.

Calliope was happy to see Kristin and baby Glow. Calliope had a special reason to find Kristin in the crowd. She wanted to talk to her about what had happened this week. There was so much to share since she had last seen her friend.

"You and Deja are sisters? That's amazing."

"I'm so sorry for your loss," she hugged Calliope and squeezed baby Glow between them.

88

Granny's letter

"My sweetheart," Cricket put his arm around Calliope's shoulder and kissed her head.

"Is it all you thought it would be?" she asked.

"I plan to do this every year. We could take this insect contest idea on the road," Cricket was wound up from the attention.

"I wanted to wait until tonight to give this to you. You were so busy today." Cricket handed her a letter that had come from Nevada. It must be from Garcia.

Calliope went into the cabin for a moment of privacy so she could see what the letter had to say.

"My Dearest Angel," the letter began.

Calliope scanned to the bottom and found the signature was not Garcia but her Granny. She looked up at Cricket who was waiting to see what the letter said.

"It's not from Garcia," she said, "it's from my Granny."

"No way," he responded, and she began to read it silently.

When I heard from Anthony that you had been to visit, I couldn't wait to write to you.

I hope you will want to see me, too. I have missed you so much and think about you every day.

I am so sorry about your mother; she had a wounded heart since she was a small girl. She never got over her father's death. I might have been wrong to keep the whole story from you as you were growing up, but I wanted to protect you from the reality of what was happening in your mother's life.

I will never forget the day I found you wading in the creek. You were the most beautiful girl I had ever seen. You were so innocent and I could see the bright spirit shine through your eyes. I had been looking for you since the day I heard you were born; I knew someone needed to look out for your welfare. I had to see if my daughter had changed, but when I saw her that day, I knew you needed to be rescued.

Calliope looked up from the letter to meet Cricket's eyes. He was waiting to see what Granny had to say.

"Is she coming for a visit?" he asked.

"She hasn't got to that yet," she replied.

"If you want to call, here's my number. Or you can write me; the address is below. If you don't want to contact me, I'll give you your space, but I want you to know, you were the brightest star in the sky of my life."

Granny

"She gave me her phone number," she handed the letter to Cricket.

He began to read it while she paced the cabin.

"Do you want to contact her?" he asked when he was done reading the letter.

"I do, of course I do. Can you get me the cell phone?" she looked up at him.

He left the letter on the table and went out to the car for the cell phone.

She was pacing when he came in with the phone. Cricket gave it to her and saw her hands were shaking as she tapped the numbers on the screen.

"Hello, Granny?" he heard her say, "It's Angel."

She looked at Cricket and smiled.

"It's good to hear your voice, too," she said.

She paced, fluttered the curtain, grabbed a paperclip off the table.

"I got your letter and I thought I'd call.

I'm doing good. Great.

I'm living in Oregon, we just moved here. How are you? Where are you?"

She saw Deja running up the walkway.

"We were just down there in Nevada."

Calliope laughed. "I guess you know that."

Deja came running up the stairs, fiddle in hand.

"Calliope! I can play 'Boil the Cabbage Down'!" Deja was yelling as she crossed the threshold.

She ran smack into Cricket who was standing just inside the doorway as the screen door banged shut.

"Well, I got married. His name is Cricket," Calliope announced.

Cricket grabbed Deja and hoisted her up, "Shh, Calliope's on the phone," he gently walked her into the bedroom and set her down.

"I can play a song!" she whispered loudly to him and held up her instrument.

"I can't wait to hear," Cricket whispered back to her.

"Can we stay another night here?" Deja asked him.

He nodded and held his finger to his lips.

"I've got my own tattoo studio," Calliope was saying. "Since we moved to Oregon, I let the other girls manage it."

"So..." she was biting her cuticle.

"Garcia told me about my mother." She stuck her hand in her pocket.

"I'm sorry, too."

Calliope shook her head. "I guess it's different when you're a kid. I never saw anything wrong with her."

"Maybe living in a tree house isn't a normal thing. But-" she grabbed a Kleenex from the table and tore it into long strips.

"My life is good now-"

"I have to tell you something. I found out I have a sister. Her name is Deja. She moved in with us last week."

Tiny nest of Kleenex on the table.

"We'll come down as soon as we can," she replied. She bit her lip and brushed tears from her eyes.

"Deja!" the little girl heard Calliope calling from the kitchen.
Deja set her fiddle on the bed and approached Calliope who was still talking on the phone.

"Okay, see you soon..."

"Someone wants to talk to you," she said, and kneeling down, she handed Deja the phone.

Glossary

The Language of Insects

ANT

COMMITMENT, INDUSTRIOUSNESS,
FAITHFULNESS

APHID

ALTRUISM

BEDBUG

SELF SUFFICIENT

BEE

WISDOM AND DILIGENCE

BEETLES

DIVINITY AND GODS

BUTTERFLIES

SYMBOL OF THE HUMAN SOUL AND MYSTERY

CADDISFLY

CONTEMPLATIVE AND SOLITARY

CICADA

MUSICAL AND LONGEVITY

COCKROACH

ANCIENT SURVIVOR

CRICKET

GOOD LUCK AND MUSICAL

DADDY LONGLEGS

COMICAL INDIVIDUALISM

DRAGONFLIES

MESSENGER OF THE GODS

EARWIG

MATERNAL NIGHT CREEPER

FIREFLY

LUMINOUS AND PLAYFUL

FLEA

MESSENGER OF DEATH, STRENGTH

FLY

DIVINE POWER

FRUIT FLY

LIFE IS FLEETING

GRASSHOPPER

GOOD LUCK AND FORTUNE, NOBILITY

HORNET

FIERCELY LOYAL

HORSEFLY

NEEDY

JAPANESE BEETLE

BEAUTIFUL MESSENGER

JUNEBUG

MISTAKEN LOYALTY

KATYDID

MUSICAL

LACEWING

STRENGTH IN BEAUTY

LADYBUG

LUCK AND BALANCE

LICE

PAY ATTENTION TO ME

LOCUST

VAGABOND MINSTREL

MAYFLY

NAIVETE

MEALYBUG

KEEPING SECRETS

MITE

CREATIVITY

MOSQUITO

CRAVE ATTENTION

MOTH

MASCULINE WISDOM

PILL BUG

SHY INTROVERT

PRAYING MANTIS

SPIRITUAL POWER

SCARAB

VIRILITY, COURAGE, STRENGTH
& RESURRECTION OF SOUL

***SCORPION**

RETALIATION, AGGRESSION, DECEITFUL

SILVERFISH

HUNGRY SOUL

***SPIDER**

CREATIVE DECEIVER

STINKBUG

CRAVES SOLITUDE

TERMITE

COMMUNITY SOLDIER

TICK

STUBBORN

WALKING STICK

SELF PROTECTION

WASP

ROYAL QUEEN

WOOLY BEAR

CONGENIAL

YELLOW JACKET

FIERCELY LOYAL

* Not an insect

Acknowledgments

My deepest gratitude goes to all my primary readers who encouraged and supported me every step of the way. And to the South Beach Writers Group who are my greatest cheerleaders. Thanks to Velta Ashbrook who gave her time and patience to my manuscript in the rough. And to Michael who spent his time, talent and energy helping me with the last push to the summit.